STALEMATE

THERE CAN BE NO WINNERS

A NOVEL

HUGO N. GERSTL

STALEMATE

THERE CAN BE NO WINNERS

A NOVEL

HUGO N. GERSTL

SAMUEL WACHTMAN'S SONS   DEKEL PUBLISHING HOUSE

STALEMATE: THERE CAN BE NO WINNERS

Hugo N. Gerstl
Copyright © 2018
Dekel Publishing House
www.dekelpublishing.com

North American rights by
Samuel Wachtman's Sons, Inc.
ISBN 978-1-941905-23-4

All rights reserved. No portion of this book, except for brief review, may be reproduced, stored in a retrieval system, or transmitted in any form or by any means – electronic, mechanical, photocopying, recording, or otherwise – without written permission of the publisher. For information regarding international rights please contact Dekel Publishing House, Israel; for North American rights please contact Samuel Wachtman's Sons, Inc., U.S.A.

Editor:	Pnina Ophir
Proofreading:	Dory Morik

Cover images:
Cotton plant farm
© Chris Boswell / Dreamstime.com

Cover design and typesetting by
DesignPeaks@gmail.com

For information contact:

Dekel Publishing House	**Samuel Wachtman's Sons, Inc.**
P.O. Box 6430, Tel Aviv	2460 Garden Road, Suite C
6106301, ISRAEL	Monterey, CA 93940, U.S.A.
Tel: +972 3506-3235	Tel: 831 649-0669
Fax: +972 6044-627	Fax: 831 649-8007
Email: info@dekelpublishing.com	Email: samuelwachtman@gmail.com

«JUSTICE, JUSTICE SHALT THOU PURSUE»

- Deuteronomy 16:20

෪ඏ

Honoring Wendy Wong, Jane Bednar, Sarah Cavassa, Kristen Cozad, Leslie Finnegan, Diana Baker, Chris Campbell, Natalie Herendeen, Jo Marie Ometer, Anne Secker, Susan Vega

෪ඏ

And, of course, for my

LORRAINE

By the same author:

Fiction

Skorzeny
The Wrecking Crew
Arcade
Assassin
Legacy
Against All Odds
Billy Jenkins
Amazing Grace
Scribe
Misfire

Non iction

The Politics of Insanity
The Politics of Hate
How to Cut Your Legal Bills In Half
The Pets Welcome™ Series

Under the Pseudonym Marvin Shapiro

How to Survive – and Profit From – Your Son's Bar Mitzvah

1945

AMERICAN SECTOR
DISPLACED PERSONS CAMP

BEULE, BELGIUM.

1

"Y'all been down here a lot lately. Y'all enjoy lookin'?"

"What means 'yawll'?" the white man asked. "Is something like this?" he asked, pointing to an awl on the workbench.

"No, that there's a *awl*," he said. "I asked whether *y'all* enjoys lookin'."

"What means? Is type of machinery?"

"Nossir. Y'all is short for 'you-all.' It's a way we say 'you' in the South, where I come from. Where you-all from, anyway?"

"*Fajsławice, Polska.*"

"Say which?"

"Is name of nearest large town to where I am born. Is in Southeast Polska – Poland I think is called in English."

"Where's that? Pol – Pol…?"

"Poland. Is far east from here. Near White Russian border? Ukrainia?"

The dark-skinned man looked at the white man suspiciously. "Y'all mean they got *two* Russias? One for white people and one for black folks like me?"

"No. Is name of country – Byelorussia – means White Russia. I think other part is called Red Russia – Soviet Union."

"My commanding officer tol' me there's a lotta' Commies there – Russia, I mean. Are you one o' them Commies?"

"What is 'Commie?'"

"Y'all don't know?" He shrugged his shoulders. "Y'all really don't know. How old are you?"

"Twenty-six."

"No shit! Me, too!" He held out his hand. "Madison Peebles."

Moses grabbed the outstretched hand – the first man to extend a hand in friendship to him since before the Nazis came. He smiled from ear to ear. "Moses Mendelssohn, like German music composer."

Madison Peebles had never heard of Felix Mendelssohn, had never even heard classical music, but he was eager to show what he believed to be the sophistication that came from having been in Europe for six months. "Does y'all speak any other languages – besides English, I mean? I suppose since you come from Polska, you prob'ly speak some Polska language?"

"A little bit of German," Moses said, looking down at the ground as if such knowledge might bring trouble.

"Hey, really?" Madison responded. "I been listenin' to the Armed Forces Radio comin' out of Germany. They've got a language program every night, and I been listenin' a coupla' times a week. I can even speak a little of their talk," Peebles said proudly. "*Sprekken... see... Dootsch?*" he asked, enunciating each word carefully, his accent abysmal.

"*Jawohl,*" Moses responded. "*Sie sprechen sehr gut Deutsch,*" he said, trying to hang onto the first thread of human bonding he'd had in years.

"You done one-upped me," Peebles said. "What does that mean?"

"It means you speak German better than I speak English," Moses said.

"Hey, no shit? Whyn't y'all stay and watch me awhile, Moses Mendelssohn? Better yet, whyn't y'all stay and keep me company?"

1989

LIBERTYVILLE, ALABAMA

U.S.A.

2

It had been fourteen years since the last really big rains had come, but this year you could tell they were coming. Maybe tonight, maybe tomorrow, but they were coming all right. As the high ground descended toward town, the trees and roots gave way to hardpack red clay, pretty-looking soil that was so poor, so leached of all nutrients that you couldn't grow anything in it except rocks. That meant only one thing. When the rains came, bigger and bigger chunks of those hills would slide down into the middle of town. The main road through town, nothing more than a dusty, fourteen-foot-wide, tamped gravel trail at the best of times, would be overrun by clay, soil, rocks, and water. Most times, the roadway would only be ankle-high in the water and red muck. Some years the stuff would be knee-high, and that's knee-high to a man, not knee-high to a duck. And sometimes, once every dozen years or so, like what portended to happen in the next day or so, there'd be days on end when, as the locals said, "You'd be up to yer ass in alligators or at least up to yer ass in water full of alligator shit."

Last time that had happened, some folks had left town for good, and not just because of the high water. Each year, times had gotten a little tougher and more folks had moved out. Twenty years ago, they closed down the lumber mill and killed off two-hundred jobs, mostly low-paying manual jobs – "Darkie jobs" they'd called them forty years ago - but if *those folks* couldn't work, they couldn't eat, and if they couldn't eat, it made no sense to stay. Then the county decided to reroute County Road 3581 through Tomkinsville, ten miles north, and they stopped paying for the maintenance of the main road into and out of town. A decade later, the granddaddy of all storms had upended the south end of town, taking down more than a hundred residences, mostly the lean-to shacks occupied by the poorest of the poor.

The Dairy Queen closed down, the Freedom Movie House shut its doors, the Kresge store sold its last dry goods, and one morning the remaining inhabitants of the town woke up to find that the Sears and Roebuck catalogue store had moved out during the night.

Every year, the signs at each end of town, the signs proclaiming, "*Libertyville – Tomorrow Starts Here!*" got a little more decrepit looking. At first, when the population slipped from 1,187 to 900, the Town Council had voted to spend a few bucks to have the town's only sign painter, Dan Alter, do a professional job on the signs' population count. Dan had died four years ago. By that time 900 had become 650, then 650 had slipped to 500. At last count, at the beginning of this year, the population of Libertyville was 278. Those people under the age of seventy who remained were moving out or trying to move their *asses* and what little *assets* they had out as soon as the breadwinner found a job anywhere else. Now, the nearest place anyone could go to get even the most basic health care was Tomkinsville.

Two months ago, a big wind had blown down the sign at the east end of town. There wasn't enough money to nail the danged thing back up. So now there was one sign, and most of *that* sign had faded, so if you drove into town you'd see a sign that said, "L b rt il e – T mor ," and below that, "Pop.," and hand-scrawled to the right of that, "1 jackass, 4 pine cones and an apple."

But you could still tell where you were, because at the western edge of town there was a three-story high structure with a huge neon sign that proclaimed, "Libertyville Cotton works."

The Libertyville cotton works had steadfastly remained the town's main employer – heck, the *only* employer left. The machinery was outdated, outmoded, and obsolete. For the past ten years at least, the crippled old gears and pulleys and belts and engines had kept running on nothing more than imagination and the genius of Madison Peebles, who'd somehow kept the machinery going long after the original manufacturers had gone out of business. Long after it became impossible to get replacement parts, even from anywhere else in the world.

But now, Madison Peebles was seventy and deaf as a post. His eyesight was going fast, and his scabrous, gnarled old hands were crippled with arthritis. It had been a year since the last major order for processing cotton had come in. Nowadays, all that business was going offshore, to Colombia and places where it cost a third of the price the Libertyville Cotton Works charged to do the job.

But, while it might seem like the end of the road for Libertyville, the clouds had a silver lining – of sorts.

ଛଓ

"You wanted to see me, Moses?"

"I did, Madison. How long have we been together?"

"Forty-five years. Been some rough ones, but lotsa' good ones, too."

"We're getting up there, my friend."

They were seated in Moses' third-floor office. The door was closed. Each of them sat quietly, sipping a snifter of brandy. The long-awaited rain had finally started coming down with a vengeance a couple hours ago. The main road past the factory was already muddy, and if the downpour kept up, it would be a bog by late tonight.

"Been thinkin' that m'self," the Black man rejoined.

CHAPTER 2

"Time for us to hang it up?"

"What're you tryin' to tell me, Moses?"

"There's no way I can make this easy, my friend. I've sold the cotton works and the land. We'll be closing it down at the end of next month."

They sat in silence for a while longer. Madison simply stirred the brandy with his forefinger, then licked off his finger when he removed it from the snifter.

"I figured it'd come sooner or later. Don't take an idiot to see business is way down. Would you tell me something?"

"Sure, Madison."

"How much we been losin' a month?"

"Three, four thousand dollars, for the past four years."

"Whoo-wee!" Madison exclaimed, then whistled. "That's almost two hunnert thousand dollars you had to write the check for."

"More or less," Mendelssohn responded.

"Man, I didn't know that kind of money existed!"

"It doesn't. Not anymore, anyway."

The African-American stood up stiffly, stretching his painful joints, made all the worse by the damp weather, and walked over to the window. He stared out at the rain toward the muddy road and sighed. Nothing either man did was done with unnecessary haste anymore. Each knew the other only had so much juice left in their weak old batteries of life, and they were trying to conserve what little they had as long as possible.

Finally, Moses said, "You thinkin' about the money part? What's gonna' happen to you?"

"Cain't say it hasn't crossed my mind," Peebles replied. "I got the Social Security and a bit of a pension in the till, unless you used part of that to help with the two hundred thousand dollars."

"No, sir," Moses replied. "Your pension's safe, Madison. Everyone else's is safe, too. The two hundred thousand came entirely out of my own pocket."

"I didn't mean anything like that, Mister Mendelssohn," Peebles said, mildly embarrassed. "I guess that's just part of what's crossin' my mind. 'Course, I ain't got nobody but me to look after, anymore, but there's nobody to look after *me*, either. 'Coupla' grandkids in Memphis, but I don't know how they're gonna' be with a half-blind, deaf old man around. I suppose I could go to one of those state homes for old people, but I've heard they're pretty ratty, some of 'em. Oh, hell, Mister Mendelssohn, let's be truthful. I don't mind any of that. It's just that I can't picture myself as *old*, even now. Hell, I've heard some of the young bucks whisperin' about 'that old fart,' and even some of 'em, when they think I can't hear, talkin' 'bout 'that old Nigger,' but in my heart I know they cain't be talkin' about me."

"Didn't we do much the same when we were younger?"

"I s'pose so. You gonna' get any part of your two hunnert thou back from the sale?"

"Depends on how long I live, my friend. Depends on how long you live, too."

"What do you mean we, White Man?" Even in this moment of profound sadness and parting, Madison chuckled softly at their thousandth replay of the cynical Lone Ranger joke, the one where the masked man and his stoic Native American friend Tonto are surrounded and about to be murdered by a horde of ferocious Indians. The Lone Ranger says, "Well, old friend, it looks like we've come to the end of the trail," and Tonto replies, "What do you mean we, White Man?"

"As part of the sale, I've made sure you're provided for." Moses reached into his desk drawer and brought out a copy of the contract to show his oldest, dearest friend. As he started to hand the papers to the man, Madison stopped him gently. "Cain't read that well and now it don't matter 'cause I cain't even see to read. Can you tell me what it says?"

"You get fifteen hundred a month, plus your Social Security, plus another thousand a month in pension fund benefits, forty-five hundred a month for the rest of your life."

Madison was stunned into silence by this unexpected bounty, more than he'd earned a month for the past decade.

"Plus, the buyer has committed to building seventy-five houses on the acreage around the factory. They've promised in writing you get to live in one rent-free for the rest of your life."

"Hallelujah and Lord ha' mercy!" Madison exclaimed. "There *is* a God after all!"

"I don't know that I can admit that yet," the white man said. "Let's just say I'm no longer so certain He doesn't exist."

"I hope you've provided for yourself."

"That I have, Madison."

"You gonna' leave the area? Ain't no place for a lonely old Kike to live, you bein' a widower and all."

"Been thinkin' that myself. It gets cold and rainy here in the winter, and that doesn't do my joints much good. My wife's family's still in Mobile. There are a lot of Jews down in southern Florida. Don't know that I'm up for travelin' anymore. More brandy, Madison?" he asked, nodding toward the bottle.

"Why not?" He moved his snifter toward his old friend. "What's gonna' happen with the others?"

"I can't see letting them down when you and I will do all right. Each of the employees will get ten thousand dollars outright, five from the pension and five from the buyer. The company that's taking over promised to allow our workers to live rent-free in those houses for twenty years or until they die or leave the area."

"Man, that is generous. They cain't ask more'n that, even on their best day. Only thing is, a lot of the workers are still pretty young. They could get into a lot of mischief with that kinda' money and nothin' to do during the day. Don't you think they'll need to find work?"

"I suppose so, Madison. But that little bit of money will give them time to do it."

"Yeah, but with the Libertyville cotton works shut down, there'll be no more money comin' into this town. That'll just accelerate the death of Libertyville."

"They could always farm the land around town."

"Yeah, but to do that, they'd have to *buy* the land. I suppose each of 'em could afford an acre, and a poor acre at that, but what d'you think they'll be able to do on that acre?"

Moses looked down at the floor, then up and around his office. "I never thought that far ahead," he said. "But, if there is a God, and these good people all seem to believe there is a God, maybe it's His turn to start thinking of what to do with 'em. Man, that rain has started to pick up, and the wind, too. Gonna' be a bum few days, maybe more."

While the two old friends had been talking, dusk had turned to twilight, and the sound of the howling wind outside contrasted with the warmth in Mendelssohn's office. Moses turned on two table lamps, which shed a warm, gentle light.

"Madison, all the while we've been I never asked you whether or not you'd like to meet your benefactor. Terry Prince, the Coast Conglomerates man, will be down here Saturday afternoon. I thought maybe …?"

"Let me think on that a little, Moses," Peebles said. "If you'll pardon an awful pun, I don't want to spook the guy and throw cold water on my bounty."

"Well, if you do, he'll be here Saturday about one o'clock, and there's no harm in you meetin' him. You got a ride home?"

"Yessir. Man named Moses Mendelssohn. But we better get outta' this place and into his car while there's still a surface for his wheels to roll on."

3

"Brother Coyle, I sure appreciate you comin' here this mawnin." The bishop, who was well capable of speaking with a cultivated Oxonian accent, a New England twang, or even, if the occasion demanded, the rich tones of the Midwest, had dropped into a deep Southern drawl in that same rumbling bass voice which had graced the airwaves over a good slice of the Southeast for more than a dozen years. "Can I git you some coffee? Sweet rolls?" He pointed expansively to a sideboard laden with sweetmeats.

"Thank you, no, Bishop Walker," the younger man responded. "It's certainly my privilege to be here," he said, with a false cheerfulness he did not feel. Both men knew exactly why Brother Augustus Caesar Coyle had been summoned to Birmingham.

The Regional Bishop of the Worldwide Church of Christ (A.M.E.) walked over to his capacious oak desk and riffled through some papers. Coyle noticed that every iron-gray hair on the Bishop's head was perfectly coiffed. His black, heavy satin robe had a rich, rubbed look with only the lightest hint of sheen, his snow-white collar enhanced his noble neck, and his magenta shawl and matching cap completed a picture of slightly overstated elegance. Bishop William Wyatt Walker, fifty-nine and six-foot three inches tall, looked every bit the powerful, high-risen churchman he was.

CHAPTER 3

And, thought Augustus Coyle, *the most arrogant bastard I've ever met. The smooth sonofabitch would sell his mother's soul or cut off his father's balls if it would further his ambition.* Bishop Walker had risen to the rarified position of Corporate Secretary of the Church – the number three man in the entire organization. It didn't matter that the church catered to some of the poorest African-Americans in the United States. What mattered more was that it catered to five *million* parishioners, plus an additional five million more who listened to the Voice of the Lord on radio stations from Texas to Alabama and from Nassau in the Bahamas to the nation's capital, and if each of these good, simple, God-fearing people put an average of one measly dollar in the collection plate each week – all of which went to headquarters, and none of which stayed in the local parish church – the annual gross came to five hundred twenty million – more than half a *billion* – dollars a year. His Excellency, the Most Reverend Bishop William Wyatt Walker, could afford to be an arrogant bastard.

"Brother Coyle, come closer, sit near to me," the Bishop said, indicating two comfortable armchairs that sat facing his desk. As he sat, Augustus noticed that the two chairs were substantially lower than Bishop Walker's executive chair. Thus, when the prelate sat, Augustus found himself gazing up at the man in front of him.

The Bishop handed one stack of papers to Augustus and kept one for himself. He appeared to be reading the documents carefully as though it was the first time he'd seen them. He spent the better part of three minutes grunting, sighing, occasionally saying, "My, my," or "That can't be." Finally he looked up at Augustus. "Brother Coyle," he said sadly, "this is not good at all. How long have you been the Pastor of our Libertyville Parish church?"

"Six years, Your Excellency."

"In all that time, the parish has never turned a profit, not one penny of profit, Brother. Now, the Lord would not be pleased, no, the Lord

Christ Jesus would not be pleased at all if He knew that it was costing us – I say *costing* the church – quite a bit of money each year to keep your parish church running."

"Your Excellency," Augustus said, a thin sheen of perspiration breaking out over his brow, "the town population has dwindled from over a thousand to two hundred seventy-eight – and that includes whites. When I came to Libertyville, we had a congregation of over five hundred."

"And today, Brother Coyle?"

"Fifty, sixty maybe."

"Fifty-seven, Brother Coyle. Ten of them are old retirees living off Social Security. Half of 'em rely on the church for a handout. What do you propose to do about the situation, Brother Coyle?"

"I don't rightly know Your Excellency. We're bringin' in four dollars a head each week, four times the national average."

"Four dollars a week!" Bishop Walker thundered. "Two hundred twenty-four fuckin' dollars a week? That's less than a thousand a month! Do you know what we pay you, Brother Coyle? *Do you?*"

"Fourteen hundred," Augustus said in a voice so low it was barely above a whisper.

"And the repairs on the church building cost?"

"Five thousand dollars so far this year."

"You've got those figures down pretty well. There's upkeep on your parish house and you gotta' feed and clothe that pretty wife of yours and those two lovely little children …"

"Yes, that's true."

"Brother Coyle, I notice there's an item here for four thousand dollars for 'Retreats and General Expenses.' That seems to be a recurring item that started in the second year after you came to Libertyville. …

CHAPTER 3

Is there something wrong, Brother Coyle? Would you like a glass of water? Perhaps something stronger?"

He rose, walked to the other side of the room, opened a door in the credenza in back of him, took out a bottle of bourbon whiskey, poured a neat shot for himself and one for Coyle. "Augustus," he said in a more confidential tone, "you and I are men of the world. We have – ah – tastes that might not seem appropriate to our God-fearing parishioners."

"I don't understand, Excellency."

"Perhaps I should make it clear. What does the name Sarah Coben mean to you?"

"How - ?"

"I'm the bishop. I know everything that goes on in my *see – everything*, do you understand? Four thousand dollars a year, Augustus. 'Retreats and general expenses?'" He tossed a packet of papers at the preacher. "Nightgowns from Intima European Apparel. A necklace from Murfrees Emporium. Flowers. Motel receipts, Augustus, all of 'em from the Royal Oak in Plattstown – checked in at noon, checked out at four p.m. It seems you done been fornicatin', Brother Coyle. Knockin' back pussy. Bangin' where you ought not to be bangin'. Polishing your pecker with that Jew-girl who lives just over the state line. The maiden lady niece of 'Ike the Kike' Mendelssohn, the old guy who owns Libertyville cotton works."

Augustus Caesar Coyle sat speechless, in stunned silence.

Bishop Walker continued, "You know, Augustus, if you throw a stone into a pond, the rings just keep spreadin' out. First, the lovely Missus Letitia Coyle learns about it, then it spreads a little more, say to the Congregation, which ain't that big a deal. But then one or two white Baptists in town hear a rumor and it keeps spreadin'. This is the South, Brother Coyle, and it's the twentieth century, but somehow that don't stop some people from nailin' a Nigger's ass to a flamin' cross if'n they get mad enough. And they *do* get mad when they learn that a black man's been dippin' into one of their own. D'you get the picture?"

Coyle looked away. His voice, when he found it, was hoarse. "Why are you doin' this, Bishop? Y'all gotta' have a reason."

"Indeed I do, son. Now all that bad stuff can come spillin' out, but maybe it don't have to."

"Wh … wh … what do you mean?"

The Bishop reached back to a humidor sitting atop the credenza. He withdrew a large cigar from the humidor, passed it under his nose in each direction, clipped one end meticulously, and lit it. He puffed contentedly for a few moments.

"Augustus, your little parish ain't worth shit to the church. It just sucks on the church's tit. And the church isn't all that bothered by your little adventures either. But your little town has something the church covets, Augustus. We want the Libertyville cotton works and the forty prime acres on which it sits. Yes, my friend, we dearly covet that little piece of earth."

"Why, sir?"

"Too many people on the outside – and a growing number of our parishioners – look upon the Worldwide Church of Christ as having departed from its small-town roots. People have lately come to associate the church with Atlanta, Mobile, Charlotte, and Jackson. And they figure if we can get that big, maybe we don't need the contributions of our flock. Indeed, Brother Coyle, our gross receipts are down six percent from last year. … Doesn't sound like much, does it, Brother Coyle?" the Bishop said conversationally, blowing several small smoke rings in succession. "D'you have any idea how much that comes to in real money?"

"No, sir."

CHAPTER 3

"Thirty-one point two *million* dollars, Brother Coyle. Enough to fund a thousand Sarah Cobens. We've simply got to return to our roots – convince the brethren that we're really, truly at one with them. We've scoured every small town in the South for the perfect place to site our new world headquarters.

"Let's not mince words, Brother Coyle. Our church feeds the souls of the masses, Brother Coyle. If you're gonna' run a McDonald's, you wanna' look like a McDonald's, you don't wanna' look like the Ritz Carlton."

"And your point is?"

"The bishops all agree that Libertyville is the perfect place. A town that once had a future, but like so many small towns in the South, all it's got now is a past. A dyin' ghost town in the makin'. Property values have fallen to nothin', the Libertyville cotton works is the last living thing in that town, and it's about to come crashin' down, Brother Coyle."

"But why do you need the cotton works? You could buy the whole town, lock, stock, and barrel for way less than ten million dollars – less than two percent of what the church brings in each year."

"Yes, Reverend Coyle, but we don't want the whole miserable town. We want the cotton works and its forty acres. The rest of the town can, you should pardon the expression, go to hell as far as the church is concerned. Except, of course, your little parish church."

"Why that place, Reverend?"

"At the end of the last World War, forty-five years ago, Libertyville was nothing but a dot on the map, a Negro outpost consisting of two hundred shacks, a county elementary school, a Flying 'A' gas station and two outhouses. About 1950, somebody got the bright idea there was lots of farmland around – good bottomland – and this would be a place to develop the future. Cotton had been king since time out of mind, but the boll weevil had attacked a lot of places in the South, so that was goin' downhill. People still needed cotton, and they'd never tried to farm it around Libertyville. And what a great name – Libertyville. It spoke of the American dream. Maybe even a place where the black man and the white man could sit down and talk.

"Well, that Jew Mendelssohn and a few others came to town, and before you know it, there really *was* a town. By 1956 the Libertyville cotton works employed three hundred fifty-two people, men and women. Let me tell you, Brother Coyle, Libertyville was hummin'. It had a population of almost two thousand by 1960, and it was the town of the future. In fact, they painted big signs saying, 'Tomorrow Starts Here!' and people believed it. The Libertyville cotton works was the symbol of all that was good, all that was great, all that was successful. It was the town's crown jewel. That place symbolized it all."

"What happened, Bishop Walker?" the younger clergyman asked, daring to take a sip of his bourbon for the first time.

"It was a false symbol, son," the prelate said. "The Libertyville cotton works was owned by a Jew. The real God, the Christian God looked down from on High and said, 'This is not right! This is not good!'" The Bishop spread his arms out expansively, the old-time preacher man very much at ease in the twenty-first century. "'That which I have raised high, I can cast into the dust,' saith the Lord. 'An abomination I shall not abide' saith He. 'Vengeance is mine!'"

The Bishop lowered his arms and the tone of his voice. "People started to leave, the price of cotton bottomed out, and the once-proud Libertyville cotton works began to fail. Today, that same Libertyville cotton works stands as a symbol to shame and failure, an icon of a people that followed money and disbelief and the false god. So, Brother, you see why the Worldwide Church of Christ looks with a caring eye on that there cotton works?"

"I'm beginning to see, Your Excellency."

"Brother Coyle, the church wants to show that the failure of the heathen can be returned to the crowning glory of the Lord. While others may boast their crystal palaces and their towers so high that their steeples stick a mote in God's eye, the Worldwide Church of Christ desires only a simple, decaying edifice to show the world its humility and its oneness with the people. Indeed, Reverend Coyle, we have no need for what people today call the 'bells and whistles,' the outer trappings of wealth and grace ..."

Augustus sucked in his breath so hard he coughed from the exertion at the rank hypocrisy of the Bishop's words. *My God, he actually <u>believes</u> that.*

The bishop continued, raising his arms like an old-time prophet. "You see, Brother Coyle, the Lord commands that that decrepit hulk, that monument to failure shall be resurrected like the Christ, and shall be the seat of our 'Worldwide Movement'!"

"Your Excellency, why does the church need the forty acres around the building?"

"Ah, son, the church intends to use the forty acres for what we will call, 'God's Country,' a place where the faithful can come and commune with each other and with God in peace. That little church where you now preach will be moved. It be the centerpiece that will stand in contrast to the monied towers of the high-risen and wealthy. And there will be places on the periphery where the faithful can stay when they spend the night with us. 'God's Inns,' we'll call them." The bishop looked directly at his subordinate. "That's where you come in, Brother Coyle."

"Me, Your Excellency?"

"Yes, and in so doing you exonerate yourself from your, ahem, misdeeds."

"How, Excellency?"

"The Lord has chosen you, the Reverend Augustus Caesar Coyle, to speak with the heathen Jew, to convince him that he must convey the property to the church."

"Why would he want to do that?"

"Because he is old, because he is tired, and because he is a failure," the Bishop said. "And because we can offer him sustenance and succor in his old age."

"In other words, you want to buy him out?"

"Yes, if, ahem, the price is right. If we can purchase the cotton works and its forty acres, the rest of the town will fall into our hands. The town can arise from the ashes like the legendary phoenix, tit can become a great city, the Lord's City."

"And the Lord's City will be owned and developed by the church?"

"Yes, son, and along with salvation, if you successfully bring this off, there will be material and ecclesiastical benefits for you as well."

"Why have you chosen me, a lowly rural preacher, when the church itself wields so much power, Bishop Walker?"

"Well … there is but one small problem in our great plan, Brother Coyle. We have learned that the heathen Jew Mendelssohn has plans to, ummm, convey the property to other, less deserving interests."

4

Night. They'd been canvassing the area for the past week. Even their seventies-vintage Plymouth with its growling mufflers and twin pipes hadn't awakened anyone. The town was a good two miles away, and people just accepted that whatever went on on the outskirts of Libertyville was none of their business. José Sandoval and Rogelio Torres had deliberately driven slowly as they approached the cotton works, so as not to arouse suspicion. There were twin lights on each side of the Libertyville cotton works sign. A single dim street lamp at each corner of the parking lot, but otherwise the place was dark.

At one-thirty, they parked the Plymouth in the woods on an abandoned fire trail and slept for the next four hours. As the sky lightened in the east, Rogelio shook his friend awake. After they'd relieved themselves under some large pines, they tiptoed quietly to a rise overlooking the cotton works. Each man wore a camouflage outfit in the unlikely event they could be seen from the factory.

Between seven and eight, a number of *Negroes* shuffled into the gates. Even by eight, there were only half a dozen cars in the parking lot. Most of those looked as careworn as the workers who emerged from them. Throughout the day, José and Rogelio could hear the clanking, the occasional screeching, but mostly the tap-tap-tapping noises that came from the cotton works. At lunch, a small number of workers came out to the parking lot and sat at four disheveled picnic tables, but most remained inside. Between three-thirty and four, the workers left and the sounds coming from the factory ceased. By four-thirty, the Libertyville cotton works was a deserted ghost town. The two Hispanics retraced their steps got in their car, and drove slowly out of the woods and back toward the place from where they'd come.

༺༻

Later that evening, in a cantina on the Gulf Coast, just over the state line, José, Rogelio, and three of their *compadres* sat in a booth toward the rear, quietly conversing.

"It's perfect for our operation," the leader, Manuel "Lobo" Cabrera said. He was forty, as far from the Hispanic stereotype as anyone could imagine. Tall, reed-thin, light-skinned, with neither beard nor moustache, he was dressed in a conservative, charcoal suit. "There's enough clanking during the day to cover any noise we might make and it's dark enough not to arouse any suspicion at night. What about the State Patrol?" He popped two Altoid mints into his mouth.

"They didn't show up once in the week we were there," Rogelio said. "Since that town is so poor, no one's gonna' rob anyone else. The only road into and outta' the place is a tar-and-gravel two-laner that gets covered in water and shit half the winter. The nearest road of any size is a good ten miles away."

"Go ahead," Manuel said.

"The gringo *Padron* looks to be a hundred years old. His partner, a deaf, half-blind old *Negrón,* looks to be a hundred-fifteen." There was raucous laughter among the five men. "If you come before seven in the morning or after five in the afternoon, they're the only ones there."

"What about the workers?"

"They'd probably run at the first sound of a rifle shot."

CHAPTER 4

"I've heard they can get pretty violent," the youngest of the group, barely out of his teens, said.

"Yeah, Roberto, if you're up in Atlanta or Philadelphia or New York they can be pretty aggressive. But down here ... well, you saw how it was with the *Negroes* in New Orleans after Hurricane Katrina. Just a bunch of dumb fuckin' sheep. It's easy to see why N'Orleans is quickly becomin' jus' like Miami and L.A. Get fifty or sixty of our riflemen into the place quickly one night. Have 'em waiting there the next morning, and whammo, we own us a neat little factory for whatever we wanna' make there – even *frijoles*," he said, laughing. "There's woods all around the cotton works. We wait quietly 'til the old *gringo* or the old *Negrón* shows up, we convince 'em it would be very unhealthy for them not to give us the key to the place, and when the *Negroes* show up, '*Adios muchachos.*' Thank you very much, don't come back."

"What if the *Negroes* go to the authorities?"

"Lobo, this is the *South*. The *last* people on earth these *Negroes* want to see are the cops."

"What about the *Señor* and his assistant?"

"Unfortunately, there are casualties in every war. I think they've lived long lives. They'd only get sicker and weaker if they had to live much longer, wouldn't you say?"

5

As she lay quietly for a few moments, vaguely enjoying his soft endearments, a constant sign of the power she had over him, she thought perhaps it was time to move on. When the vibrator felt better than the man, that was always a sign that the affair had peaked and was now on the downhill slide.

Augustus – A.C., she called him – was an ardent, if not sophisticated, lover. He was neither jealous nor threatening. She knew going into the relationship that he'd never leave his wife and children, and that was just fine with her. The attachment was straightforward and centered on one thing.

Sarah Coben, five-foot-seven, and stately, with straight dark hair, generally wore little, if any, makeup, and made it a point to dress in such a way that she wouldn't attract unwanted attention. She rarely, if ever, wore heels, but she wasn't one of those Tevas or Birkenstock types. When she slept alone at night, she wore flannel pajamas or tee-shirts rather than flimsy nightgowns or lingerie.

In the old days, one might have called the thirty-seven-year-old woman a spinster or a maiden schoolmarm. Sarah had never married – by choice – but referring to her as a *maiden* was terminally inaccurate, as many of her lovers over the years could attest. Indeed, for all her bookish looks, her doctorate degree from Bryn Mawr, and her well-paid and prestigious position as a full professor of medieval and

CHAPTER 5

romance history at Barrymore State University, Sarah Coben was a consummate sexual athlete, who'd left many former lovers wondering why she'd tired of them.

Augustus Coyle was a handsome man, and although she'd felt her ardor cooling during the last few months, he was a good one. She felt him tense under her hand, not from the immediate need for more sex.

"What's bothering you, A.C.?"

"A lot."

"Define 'a lot.'"

"The church has been spying on us, Sarah."

"I'm not surprised," she said.

"You're taking it rather calmly. Doesn't it bother you that our careers could come crashing down? After all …"

"I know, my dear," she said almost patronizingly. "I'm white, you're black, I'm a high-positioned Jewess and you're a married preacher man."

"It's not funny," he said, irritation creeping into his voice. "You're 'free, white, and over twenty-one,' educated, with a high-paying job, and you could get another position halfway across the country with no trouble at all. You're not the one who's trapped."

"I'm not joking, A.C.," she said more seriously. "You're a bright man and a good one. You're trapped in a little shit-excuse for a dying town, where you're probably taking home twice what your church brings in a year. Unless I miss my guess, that's about twelve hundred a month."

"Fourteen."

"Fourteen then. In the year of Our Lord nineteen eighty-nine. two thousand sixteen. A.C., I hate to tell you this, but with your education, your charm and, let's not kid ourselves, your good looks, you could be making three times that amount without too much effort. And you'd be appreciated. Have you ever once considered the opportunities available to you? I don't mean in a Podunk hole like Libertyville and, forgive me, Your Holiness, I don't mean in the Worldwide Church of Christ A.M.E. Put you in Philadelphia or Kansas City, run you for city council, maybe after that for Congress, and you'd have it made in the shade."

"Sarah, if I told you something very private, very personal, could you keep it to yourself?"

"No, of course not. I'm going to place a full-page ad in the *Times-Picayune.*"

"Can't you be serious for one moment?"

'"You wanted to know if I could be serious, and if I could keep a secret. I would think you'd know the answer by now. Your high-and-mighty church elders, who, if they're young enough, probably screw their brains out when they're a hundred miles from home, are obviously trying to make a big deal about you playing around a little bit. For all I know, they've threatened you with excommunication or at the very least, disclosure, but let me tell you something. They're in no great rush to replace someone with charisma who'll work seven days a week for twenty-four thousand a year, with maybe a little more for the extracurricular activities. They may or may not tell Letitia, but being a woman myself, I can tell you she'd probably forgive you. What else is she gonna' do and who else can she run to?"

"That has nothing to do with the secret."

"OK," she said, raising her right hand. "I promise that if you tell me your big, dark secret, I will not disclose what you say outside this motel room unless you want me to, and frankly, my dear, if you choose not to tell me, it's not the end of the world."

"Sarah, what if I told you I'd been offered a promotion? A really big one?"

CHAPTER 5

"Great. Who do you have to kill?"

"I don't. How close are you with your uncle Moses?"

"Not."

"That's a rather direct answer."

"It's a truthful one, A.C. Moses Mendelssohn's late wife was my mother's older sister. The family always thought Aunt Leah jumped off the edge of the earth when she left Mobile and went to live in, you should pardon the expression, your fair town. I wasn't even born then. We didn't see her except maybe once or twice a year, and occasionally when someone got sick or someone died. We always thought Moses was a bit standoffish. Not that he acted as though he was better than any of us – probably the reverse was true. You have to understand, he was a Holocaust survivor. He just wasn't what you'd call possessed of polite society social skills."

"You left Mobile."

"Different story. I wasn't exactly a JAP – Jewish American Princess – because I didn't really look the part. I was neither small, nor cute, nor *zaftig*, but the family struggled hard to get me to go to a northeastern university, and when I made it to Bryn Mawr, well, that was big *yiches* – a great honor – a heck of a lot more than any member of the family had done in the past."

"So you dislike your uncle Moses."

"No. You asked if we were close, and I answered you truthfully. We don't love one another and we don't hate one another. I'd say we're mostly indifferent to one another. The old saying, you can choose your friends, but you can't choose your family seems appropriate. Our paths simply don't cross, and since Aunt Leah passed, we really don't have any reason to have them cross."

"What do you know about the Libertyville cotton works?"

"Not much. The few times I've seen it, I wasn't that impressed."

"D'you know anything about your uncle's plans for it?" "Not really, A.C. I heard he was offered some pretty serious money for it by some conglomerate out of Atlanta, but that's a third-hand rumor. Why do you ask?"

"Well … this is the secret … and the key to my promotion, whatever that means. The church wants that particular piece of property, including the old cotton works, really badly. They want to set up worldwide headquarters there, complete with a religious theme park …" As he explained the church's plan to her, her eyes widened, but underneath her apparent fascination, her mind was working coolly, thinking ahead.

"You say they want to take over the forty acres, then take over the whole town, then the entire countryside?"

"Something like that. Who knows? They might be angling for their own miniature nation. The farmland surrounding Libertyville is fertile enough once it's used for something other than cotton."

"I suppose. But if – I said *if* – my uncle has contracted to sell the forty acres, your church is a 'day late and a dollar short.'"

"Not necessarily. Contracts can be broken."

"What about simply going to the buyer and trying to cut a deal?"

"Wouldn't work," he said, rising and pulling back the curtain to gaze briefly into the parking lot. "Any developer would realize they're getting a once-in-a-lifetime deal and they'd jack the price up to astronomical heights."

"And your church couldn't afford it?"

"It's not a question of afford, Sarah. They're looking to bring Christ to the multitudes, and make big bucks in the process. The bishop indicated they're looking for rapid development of an underdeveloped property – translation, buy low, sell high. They believe they could do better by going one-on-one with Moses Mendelssohn."

"Or 'Ike the Kike' as I'm sure your bishop calls him," Sarah said sardonically. "You don't know him, though, A.C. From the rare dealings I've had with him, he's a tough nut to crack. Did you know he's a Holocaust Survivor? You keep glancing at your watch. It's only three thirty."

"I was just thinking it'd be nice if I got home early."

"Feeling guilty?"

"Sometimes I really do. This is just one of those days. "

"Uncle Moses survived the Holocaust by sheer force of his will. Not much left but his almighty honor. He says he doesn't give a damn if there's a God or not. That means if – *if* – he signed on the dotted line, twelve saints singing Hosannas and twelve bishops wearing their most impressive finery aren't going to move him off his position."

"So what do you suggest?"

"Tell the bishop the truth. There's got to be fifty 'Libertyville cotton works' in some dying town in the Southeastern quadrant of the good ole' U.S.A. Cheap cotton works. Available cotton works. Cotton works that aren't owned by a Jew so stubborn he'd cut off his nose to spite his face if he thought his honor was at stake."

Augustus looked at the floor, despondent. "Win it, I win everything, lose it, I'm history, my marriage is history, my future is history."

"A bit melodramatic, wouldn't you say? I didn't say it was impossible. I just said 'if.' What've you got to lose by visiting him and discussing it with my uncle? The best time would probably be a Saturday morning. He sure as hell doesn't observe the Sabbath, but his employees certainly do, and your flock doesn't gather 'round 'til Sunday."

"Well, thank you, I guess," Augustus said, donning his light windbreaker and heading toward the door. "Same time next week?"

"I'm literally blown away by how wonderfully romantic you are, A.C. Oh, don't get upset, I'm just teasing. Whatever else we've got, we certainly have one thing going for us. You be on your way. I'll spend some time watching the first half of *Oprah* and I'll still be able to get to my meeting on time."

ಸಿಂ

"Mister Mendelssohn? This is Reverend Augustus Coyle, from the Worldwide Church of Christ."

"Is it that time of the year again?" Moses asked gruffly. "I gave you people two hundred dollars six months ago."

"And we humbly thank you for it, Sir. But that's not why I'm calling. Is there a time you and I could get together to talk privately, just the two of us?"

"Why would you want to talk to me?" he guffawed. "If you're looking for a convert, you've come to the wrong place. You'd be like a chicken pecking around an empty yard."

"No, Sir. This is about something that might be of great benefit to you."

"Are you telling me I've won the raffle or something?"

"No, a bit more serious than that."

"What then?"

"I'd rather tell you face-to-face. Could we meet at your place, say, Saturday morning? It'd probably be the one time and place where we could have some privacy."

"Well, ordinarily I sleep in on Saturday. What time did you have in mind?"

CHAPTER 5

"Ten-thirty?"

"Works for me."

☙❧

Moses had been off the line less than an hour when Bruce Greenbaum, his lawyer, called him from Atlanta. "Bruce, to what do I owe the pleasure of this call – and before you say anything, I'm having what the television commercials call 'acid reflux' this morning."

"Just a short call to let you know we delivered the signed contract last night, so the deal's closed and under way."

"Great – I think. How long is escrow?"

"Thirty days. Coast Conglomerates wants to send their area rep, Terry Prince down to look over the place. They don't want to be obvious about it, so they thought the best time to come would be on a weekend, when the cotton works are shut down."

Moses stared at the Week-at-a-Glance calendar on his desk. "This Saturday's probably as good as any. I promised the local preacher I'd meet him here at ten-thirty. I'm sure what he has to say won't take more than half an hour, so if Mister Prince wants to drop by, say, one o'clock or so, there won't be anyone around and I can stay out of his way."

"Great, Moses! I'll call Coast back now and firm it up."

6

At seven-thirty that evening, a very demure, conservatively dressed Sarah Coben knocked on the door of the Rabbi's quarters, a mile from the university campus. She heard the hearty, deep voice of Mordechai Ben Zvi call out, "Just a moment. Sarah, is that you?"

"Yes, Rabbi."

"I'm right here." The door opened and she stood face to face with the *Rebbe*. Mordechai was her own age, tall, with the full beard and *payess*, the traditional earlocks, of the Orthodox Jew. Most striking about him were his gentle demeanor, and the kindest, wisest brown eyes she'd ever seen. When he looked at her, his gaze was direct. He didn't try to avoid her eyes, like so many men did, and, so far as she could tell, he did not project the least bit of sexual desire for her. Of course, this, coupled with the fact that she found him extraordinarily sexy, made him that much more of a challenge.

"Come on in. I've got nothing better to offer except tea and a day-old sugar cookie."

"That's okay. I brought Kosher honey cake." As Sarah stepped across his threshold, she surveyed the place. The living room was small and very neat. The most notable thing in the room was a floor-to-ceiling bookcase filled with books. There was no hint of a feminine hand anywhere. No flowers, no frills.

CHAPTER 6

It had been their custom since Mordechai ben Zvi had arrived at Barrymore State, to visit with one another for an hour or so each Wednesday night. Sometimes they met in the university cafeteria, other times in the faculty lounge. Tonight he'd suggested she come to his home. "A little more private and not so many heads would turn or gums would flap," he'd said. She felt remarkably comfortable in Ben Zvi's presence. Their conversations seemed neither forced nor strained. It was clear he viewed her as a friend or a sister, nothing more, and she could live with that, for now.

Within the first month she learned he was a widower. Other than that, ben Zvi was circumspect about his life. He didn't wear his status as a badge of pride, nor of some incalculable wound. He simply concentrated on other things. Although she'd often felt like touching him, even squeezing his hand, she knew enough about the Orthodox Jewish traditions that she did not dare touch him. It was strictly forbidden for a man and woman who were not married to touch one another, even in friendship.

Ten minutes after she'd entered the house, she was seated in an alcove off a kitchen that was substantially smaller than the living room. Ben Zvi brought two empty mugs, a small metal teapot, the honey cake, a knife, two forks, and two small plates, on a serving tray, and sat across from her. "I hope you don't think I invited you over here to try to seduce you. It's just that meeting in a public place just to talk inanities was so sterile, so artificial. We could have gone on talking about the weather, the student loads we're carrying, the faculty and administration, and whatnot, and ten years into the friendship, we'd still know little more about each other than we did three days after we met."

"I know the feeling, Mordechai. Talking about everything and talking about nothing. Have you ever heard of the *Professor Doctor von Igelfeld Entertainments?*"

"Can't say I have."

"They're three of the funniest books I've ever read. They're by Alexander McCall Smith, a professor over in Scotland."

"McCall Smith? The guy who wrote *The Number One Ladies Detective Agency?*" he said, his eyes lighting up.

"The same. You mean you don't just read those heavy-duty Hebrew Scriptures in your living room?"

He laughed out loud. "That's the Seventeenth Century view of Hasidic Jews," he said. "We live in the twentieth century. That means that even among us 'observant Jews' adjustments have to be made. You said *Von Igelfeld?*"

"Yes. There are three books about Professor Doctor Moritz-Maria von Igelfeld and his two colleagues at the Institute of Romance Philology. The three of them jockey for position at their university, they go on holiday together, they've been each other's closest acquaintances for fifteen years, yet they're so stiff and formal toward one another it really keeps the humor going."

"And?"

"They remind me in a funny way – funny and sad – about what you just said. People know each other for years, work together for years, yet they know less about one another than they do about the girl at the checkout stand in their local supermarket."

He cut a fairly large slice of the cake, then cut it in two widthwise, placed one of the half-slices on each plate, and passed the larger half over to Sarah.

"Mordechai," she said, "I'll take your word for it that you didn't invite me over to seduce me. I hope you didn't invite me over tonight to convert me to your brand of Judaism."

"Not at all. I have my fill of doing that all day long, whenever I'm supposed to be the *Rebbe* at the Chabad House and *Rabbi* at the campus Hillel organization." He held his hands up, palms out toward her. "'Scout's honor' to use a mixed metaphor," he said. "I really invited you over tonight just so we could talk. Two people, each a universe unto ourselves, passing within close enough proximity that we can try to make life a little more pleasant for the other, so that each of us might legitimately feel another person cares."

"That's lovely, Mordechai. Something from the Talmud?"

"Nope. Something from salesman's school."

"*Salesman's school?*" she said, laughing. "Is that what they teach Chabad rabbis? Is that why you guys are so successful?"

"Hardly," he said. He poured each of them a cup of steaming black tea. "Milk or lemon?"

"Plain, please. What do you mean 'hardly?'"

"I was about as far from being a man of the cloth as you can get," he said. "I was raised in a Reform Jewish home on Long Island. So reform we even had a 'Chanukah Bush' every Christmas. I did the 'nice Jewish boy' thing, graduated Princeton, went into advertising, married the right girl."

"I'm glad we're finally getting to that. You never talk about it, and that makes you a little bit like Mount Everest, tall, lonely, and silent."

"It's not a pretty story. I'm not the type to trouble others with my problems."

"Trouble me," she said seriously.

"I married Sylvia when I was twenty-three and she was twenty-one, perfect. We'd met at the university and followed our hearts and our hormones, not necessarily in that order, into marriage. The first couple of years were the happiest I can remember, even to this day. We constantly teased each other about how gorgeous our kids would be."

Sarah sat silently, listening as he continued.

"After three years, we decided the time was ripe for kids. So we tried for a year, but nothing happened. One day a friend who'd gone to med school, suggested we go to a fertility clinic for reassurance. I talked about it with Sylvia, and it was really embarrassing, but finally we decided to go and get tested." He coughed uncomfortably.

"Problem?" she asked.

"I'll be all right. The doctor called Syl back a few days later and said he wanted to re-do the Pap smear. Sylvia'd never had a Pap smear before and she'd remarked how surprisingly unintrusive it was. Two days after the second Pap smear, he asked us both to come in together. The report was not at all what we'd expected. Cervical cancer. It had spread to the secondary stage and metastasized. Within a week, he'd gotten Sylvia into Memorial Sloan Kettering. She hung on for ten months. She believed to the very end she'd beat it. She was twenty-six."

"Oh, my God!" Sarah said.

"That was nine years ago," he continued.

"I don't know what to say."

"I didn't know what to say or do either. First thing I went on one hell of a bender, but, would you believe it, I have some kind of enzyme I'm told is a Jewish trait: I get deathly sick to my stomach if I have more than a glass of wine. Cry? You'd better believe it. My throat got so raw I imagined I'd contract throat cancer and join Sylvia quickly. Didn't work. Then, one day, the Jewish chaplain at Memorial Sloan Kettering stopped by my apartment and brought me a copy *When Bad Things Happen to Good People*, a book by Rabbi Kushner, whose son was born with a genetic disease that caused him to age at four times the speed of a normal human being. The book helped a little, not much, but it was a beginning."

"Mordechai, I'm so sorry. I didn't know."

CHAPTER 6

"How could you possibly know, Sarah? It was almost a decade ago in a city more than a thousand miles away. It's not your burden, and I feel ashamed I'm unloading it on you."

"You want to talk some more?"

"If you don't mind."

"I certainly don't," she said, involuntarily reaching out her hand, then drawing it quickly back as she recognized she might be overstepping the bounds of his propriety.

"I'd heard that Chabad, the Orthodox Hasidic Jews, did 'grief' very well. I'd always had a contrary view of the sect. They'd managed to get really bad press from the entrenched American Jewish establishment. They were wild animals who had strange beliefs and stranger habits. They didn't play ball by establishment rules, they were noisy and abrasive, and they didn't try to fit into Christian America. To the contrary, they not only aggressively proselytized, but if a Jewish man wanted to marry a Gentile woman, or vice versa, they didn't turn their back on such a union as the establishment did, but they actively went out to convert the non-Jewish partner to Judaism. Small wonder the Jewish establishment turned their back on them, or, worse yet, condemned them. It was the flip side of the Jews-for-Jesus coin – a highly centralized, Messianic brand of Judaism focused on a single leader, the *Rebbe*, Menachem Mendel Schneerson. But since Chabad was taking serious numbers of adherents and serious money away from the Reform and the Conservative Jews, Chabadniks were anathema."

"And you found?"

"Like people anywhere, there were good people and 'less good people,' but they didn't condemn me for my past. Their idea was, 'First, let's help him come back to life, then let's help him come back to his Jewish roots.'"

Sarah stood up and stretched. "Shall we adjourn to the living room? I hate to complain, but hard wooden chairs have about the same comfort level as hard cafeteria chairs."

"Sure," he said. "We can even continue drinking tea in the living room."

"No pictures of Sylvia?" she asked.

"Oh, there are many stuffed away in photo albums, but the only photo I carry is the one in my heart."

"You say they brought you back to life?"

"They did. Largely by giving me the space I needed and the consolation I wanted. After a while, I thought, 'Hey, maybe there's something to this.'"

"So you became a Rabbi?"

"Well, yes and no. *Rebbe* loosely translates into 'teacher.' Have I been ordained by any traditional sect? No. Does the hierarchy consider me a heretic? Probably. I'm sure I'm a little too liberal for them. But I've done the surface-correct things. Three years ago I changed my name to Mordechai ben Zvi."

Sarah's eyes widened. "That wasn't your birth name?"

"Mark Davis. That's the name you'll find on every document associated with my identity."

"Mordechai from Mark I can understand, but ben Zvi?"

"'Ben' means 'son of.' My dad's name was Darren, for which there's no exact Hebrew translation. He played quarterback on his high school football team and they nicknamed him 'the antelope,' which is a kind of deer. The nickname stuck. Zvi means 'deer' in Hebrew. So I became Mordechai, the son of the deer. But enough of me, Sarah. Turnabout's fair play. Have you ever been married? Kids?"

She turned and faced him directly. "Neither, Mark – or Mordechai, which do you prefer?"

"Either's fine. I'm not going to ask …"

"The not married part's my own choosing, and, no, since the question will come up sooner or later, I am not a virgin.."

"A gentleman friend?"

"Ask me no questions and I'll tell you no lies. If you mean a love-of-my-life romance like you obviously had with Sylvia, the answer's no. Do you want to teach Jewish Studies and be the token rabbi at a small university for the rest of your life?"

"Do you want to teach history at a small university for the rest of *your* life?"

"Touché. It pays the bills, it justifies my existence, and it gives me a great deal of freedom. There's actually a reason I asked the question. Rumor around the campus has it you'd like to start some kind of commune."

"I'd hardly call it a commune. I'd like to do what the Rubashkin brothers did, before they got too big and self-important."

"The Rubashkin brothers?"

"Postville, Iowa?"

"Doesn't ring a bell."

"Okay, long story short. In 1987 a pair of young orthodox Jewish brothers bought a defunct slaughterhouse in Postville, a dying town of a thousand people in northeastern Iowa. Their idea was to turn the place into a processing plant for strictly Kosher meat. They came with a few friends. Of course, all of them were married, Most of them had two or three babies already. The men wore beards and earlocks, they dressed in long black gabardines and black homburg hats, even in the middle of summer. Their women were clothed head to foot so you could hardly see an inch of skin, they did the whole Jewish *shtick*. They were a stereotype straight out of *Fiddler on the Roof*. If two dozen

Martians had come down to earth in the middle of an Iowa cornfield – Martians who were completely insular and wanted nothing to do with the local populace – you'd be pretty close to the reception these people got. It was not a scene out of *The Music Man*.

"The two communities lived side by side, studiously ignoring each other for some years. Then, something very funny happened. Agriprocessors, the name of the Rubashkin brothers' business, started to be successful and then it started to *really* grow. They processed Kosher meat, but then they expanded and had a side of the factory where they processed non-Kosher meat. Within ten years, they simply didn't have enough orthodox Jews in Postville to handle the business. And Postville, Iowa was not Brooklyn, New York, so you didn't have Jews clamoring to go live there. Too much business, too few Jews. Something had to give.

"Well, something did give, and it was beautiful. The Rubashkins started hiring gentiles, and while the two groups didn't go so far as to socialize once the workday was over, they started talking with one another and they found out they all suffered from the same disease – they were all human beings. Postville went from a population of a thousand to a population of twenty-five hundred. Fourteen different nationalities worked in the Agriprocessors plant. Seven hundred people, almost half of the town's workforce.

"At its zenith, Agriprocessors bought and sold one hundred million dollars' worth of livestock a year. They were the biggest Kosher meat supplier in the country. But then they changed their initial direction. They started cutting costs by hiring Mexican *illegals*. They paid them poorly, working conditions were horrendous, and …"

"All in the name of profit."

"Yep. Ultimately they got into a world of hurt, civil and criminal. They've been banging through the bankruptcy court for years."

CHAPTER 6

"And you'd like to replicate the way they were when they started?"

"In principle, yes. I'm way too squeamish to operate a slaughterhouse, but I was thinking, what about eggs? Everyone had to eat something. Why couldn't we raise hens, process and ship eggs??

"Where would you get the money to make it work?"

"I'm sure money would come in. At least I hope money would come in. Mostly, I'd like to see a place where people can work together toward a goal – all kind of people, Jews, African-Americans, Hispanics, white Christians, Muslims, just to show it could be done."

"That all sounds so utopian. My uncle pulled it off – for a while, anyway. If you want your 'dying town,' Libertyville's certainly that. A lot of land, probably very cheap. If not Libertyville, there are dozens of Libertyvilles all over the South. Is money really an issue?"

"Not really. More *ennui* than anything else. One routine day leads to another and before you know it, nine years have gone by. *Gan Sylvia* I'd like to call it. Sylvia's Garden."

As he saw her out the door, Sarah thought, *You may not know it, you lovely, lovely man, but I'm going to push you and prod you until you make this dream of yours happen.*

7

"We'll start tomorrow night," Cabrera said. "We don't need to send everyone in yet. Maybe a dozen in four cars. We'll send the van in first. That'll give us enough food to last for at least a week. Starting Monday, we'll consolidate our position."

Outwardly José shared his friends' euphoria. It would be a Hispanic beachhead, one of the first in the small-town South. A dream come true and they wouldn't have to share it with the fuckin' Haitians or the Holier-than-thou stinkin' rich Cubanos who'd come to Miami when Batista fell and had lived and prospered there forever. The Cubanos who spat on the Manuel Cabreras of the world, and who acted like their shit didn't stink. As if the way they'd made their money was better than the Mexicans', or their fancy women were a better grade of human being than those of his compadres.

"Let's go over the plan one more time, *lider*," Rogelio said.

"First the van. Then, I'll drive the first of two cars to the outskirts of town shortly after three in the morning. José will drive the second car. The next two cars will follow an hour later. The *muchachos* will come in from the woods carrying rifles. The food van will be parked off the road. The first order of business will be to unload the food and get it inside. The wind and rain will cover what sounds they make."

"What if the gate is locked?" This from José.

CHAPTER 7

"It probably won't be," rejoined Rogelio. "It wasn't when we last explored the site. The bigger problem might be a locked door or a watchman."

"If there's rain, there won't be a watchman," Cabrera said. "If there's a padlock, we'll cut it off with the pipe cutter. There are enough windows at ground level we can kick one of them out. Whoever gets in first opens the door from the inside to let the others in. They can always blame the rain or the wind or the old age of the windows. I don't expect anyone'll be there before Monday morning at the earliest. By then we'll have another couple dozen troops inside the building."

"Where will the men sleep?"

"Anyplace they can find a spot," Cabrera said. "Our guards will be in place no later than eight o'clock Saturday morning."

ಉ೦ಬ

"Excellency, Augustus Coyle here."

"Yes Brother Coyle?" the rich, reverberant voice purred over the line.

"I'm meeting Mister Mendelssohn at the plant Saturday morning at ten-thirty."

"Convince him, any way you can. Say what you have to say – we've been over the script. You might have to part with some of the church's money, that's okay, too. The church represents thirty of the seventy workers at that factory. We can close it down if we have to, while he thinks about our offer. Don't forget, Augustus, there's a huge, stake in your future if you bring this off, and a great big pit to fall into if you don't."

8

The rain kept up, unabated, all day Friday. Just after dark, the rain slowed to an occasional shower, but a fresh wind kicked up. To add to the problem, at least a dozen of the smaller trees and one or two of the larger ones had come crashing down near the main road. If history was any guide, the road into and out of Libertyville would be completely impassable by midnight.

"Looks like one of those 'Up to yer ass in alligator shit' years," an old timer, who was sitting in a nineteen-fifties-style counter at Ruby's, said to his neighbor.

"Yeah," the other man remarked. "I'd hate to be stuck down in Darktown tonight. I imagine half their shacks'll be gone by mornin'. Shame, Jarrod. That'll cut the number of people left in this town by half again."

"D'ya hear anything more about the rumor that Mendelssohn sold out and they're gonna' shut down the factory?"

"Can't say I have. 'Course since I get my Social Security check each month, m' house is paid for, I got food in my belly, and the old truck still runs, I don't really give a shit if this whole place goes to hell in a handbasket. It sure isn't gonna' kill me if I lose the few bucks I get each week as a night watchman over at the cotton works."

"That's not very patriotic, Roy," Jarrod said, jovially poking the other's huge stomach, which protruded a good two inches over his belt buckle.

CHAPTER 8

"Don't really care if it's patriotic or not. I done enough for this town when I was younger. Now all I want to do is live out the rest of my days in peace, just like you. B'sides, every time you turn around, another of our buddies has kicked the bucket. Who knows how much time we got left?"

"You workin' tonight?"

"Hell, no. You think I'm gonna' bust my ass standing guard on a rainy Friday night in this shit when the only ones I'd have to guard are the rats and the rabbits? Not hardly. B'sides, old Madison Peebles, the head Nigger, told me I didn't have to come in tonight." He stood up, grabbed his XXL-size coat and battered cowboy hat from the rack. "I'm goin' home to the wife. See ya' Monday night if we're still alive."

ಸಾಡ

Hector Resendiz, the youngest man in the advance cadre was driving the first vehicle, a beige Chevy van filled with a week's worth of food and a case of Altoid mints. Rogelio Torres had told him they'd need all the food in the van as well as the Coleman stoves, the soap, and the other supplies because they'd be like an invading army in a hostile land. They would not be able to depend on the locals for anything.

He and Francisco had loaded up the van until it didn't seem it could carry another thing. They'd gassed up the Chevy van fifty miles ago.

"How much farther, *amigo*?" Francisco asked.

"I don't know, man," Hector answered. "There's supposed to be a cutoff road to the right, ten miles north of State twenty-seven. From there, another twelve miles to the factory."

"I think I see a cutoff up ahead." Francisco laughed. "As if I could see fifty feet ahead of us in this friggin' rain."

"Yeah, and the front window's startin' to fog up," Hector said. "We gotta' slow down a bit. You'd think they'd have checked the defroster on this baby to make sure it was workin'." He cracked the window a bit. "Cold as a witch's tit out there."

"How would you know, Hector? You been with a witch lately?"

"Only my woman, and I can tell you there's nothing cold there," he chuckled knowingly.

They drove a mile farther until they saw a cutoff road on the right. As they turned off the paved highway, the van mushed and its footing became sluggish. "If we have to go through twelve miles of this stuff it could take us three hours," Hector groused.

"Wanna' pull off to the side for a few minutes?"

"Nawww, I'm not that chickenshit," Hector said. "Let's just keep pluggin' away."

Two miles further in, Hector was barely able to stop the van just ahead of a tree that had fallen in the middle of the road. "Shitfuck!" he exploded. The two men got out of the van and stood for a minute in the pelting rain, surveying the situation. "The tree's not as big as it looked from inside the truck," Hector said. "We could jiggle it a little way. There's a six foot wide clearing, and if we can move the tree a couple of feet, maybe…"

The two men strained mightily at the tree. After five minutes, they were able to dislodge it to the extent that the van could make it – barely – around the trunk. The branches might scratch up the side panels, but that was just tough. Francisco stood outside the truck, directing Hector. The van had just about made it around the tree when the right rear tire started churning the muck, trying to make purchase. It didn't grab the road. Hector got out of the vehicle again, swearing mightily.

"Let's try and rock it," Francisco suggested. "Probably the only way to get this fucker moving again." Hector ripped a few smaller branches off the tree and stuffed them under the right rear tire, hoping to give the van some minimal traction. Neither man observed that the van was sitting atop a series of roots that had become exposed and loosened by the constant rain. Nor could they have anticipated a sharp crack of lightning that hit the unsteady tree a moment later.

Whether or not they had been able to anticipate what was coming really made no difference. The tree buckled, then fell onto the van's hood. Hector and Francisco might have survived, had not Hector left the engine running. Within minutes, the two men, the van, and the food were a single charred mass.

༄༅༄

Manuel's first indication something might be wrong came when the car he was driving arrived at the cutoff and he found flashing red and blue lights blocking the side road. Nearby, a man in a poncho got out of a state patrol cruiser and approached him.

"Something wrong, Officer?" he asked politely.

"The road's closed all the way to Libertyville. Some trees came down, then there was a lightning strike that started a small forest fire. They'll have it under control in a few hours."

"Is there another way into town, Officer? My aunt needs medical help. I understand there's no doctor left in Libertyville."

The patrolman looked over the car, a late model Ford Taurus, "You're not from these parts?"

"No, sir. Henderson, seventy-five miles south of here."

The officer scratched his head for a moment. "I'll go back to the patrol car and check on road conditions in the area." He returned to his vehicle and punched in the license number of the Taurus, just as a routine check to make sure there was nothing unusual. The car was registered to Sunlite Industries, Incorporated, with a Henderson address. Nothing suspicious. He wrote a few entries on a blank piece of paper and returned to Manuel's car. "Boy, what irony," he remarked.

"What do you mean, officer?"

"Here it is raining cats and dogs and you guys work for a company called Sunlite."

Manuel was caught off guard for a split second. The guy from whom he'd borrowed the car hadn't said anything about any Sunlite Industries. The patrolman continued, making friendly conversation. "What d'you guys do at Sunlite?"

Manuel Cabrera was no dummy. His sensitive antennae caught that the guy must have checked for the car's registration when he'd gone back to the patrol vehicle. He had no idea who in hell Sunlite Industries was, but he'd have to gamble the cop didn't know anything about the company either. "We import oranges from Mexico, officer. I'm the shipping manager. My two co-workers and I got off work six hours ago. Luckily, it's a weekend. We don't have to work tomorrow or Sunday, so we can hopefully get my Aunt Anna down to Henderson before Doctor Sharp goes out for his two o'clock round of golf."

"Golf? In this weather?" The patrolman looked suspicious for the first time.

"Yeah," Manuel said, grinning. "It's still dry as a piece of cardboard down in Henderson. Even if it wasn't, Doc Sharp would go out with his Saturday foursome. Go figure."

The patrolman relaxed. "Best way to get to Libertyville is to go up twenty point six miles to County Road 3581, then cut east to Tomkinsville, about seven miles from the main highway. When you get there, you'll find the local road down to Libertyville. In rain like this, that road is always in questionable condition, but so far we've received no reports it's closed. You'll come into town from the east. Do you know the town well enough to find where your aunt lives?"

"How many Anna Galbas you think live in that town, officer?"

"You're not a Mexican, then?"

"No, sir. I said the *company* imports oranges from Mexico. I'm from Madrid, Spain. I am Maximilian Bragado-Galba y Alcantar," he said, showing the officer a forged California driver's license, and using an alias he'd employed many times.

"That's quite a mouthful," the patrolman said. "Well, good luck to you Mister Alcantar. Hope you find better weather toward Libertyville, but I doubt you will."

ಸಿ⚭

It was six in the morning by the time the four cars reached the rendezvous spot in the woods overlooking the cotton works. They were more than two hours behind schedule. It would be daylight in less than an hour. The supply van was nowhere in sight, which was odd, because it had started out a good hour ahead of him. The only thing José could surmise was that Hector had probably become confused when he found the cutoff road closed and the young man would probably have had smarts enough to wait until daylight to find his way to Libertyville. Still, José's stomach was growling already. If nothing else, he'd have liked a cup of hot coffee.

"Looks like your bright young kid couldn't find his way in the dark," Rogelio smirked.

"He'll be along, I'm sure," José replied.

"OK, guys," Manuel said quietly. "We've got no time for small talk. It's five hundred yards to the factory. The rain seems to have let up for the moment. We'd better get our butts into that building before daylight. *Andalé*, let's go!"

The men slogged through the mud as quickly and quietly as they could, holding their rifles above their heads. When they got to the tarmac, Manuel was relieved to find the gate was not locked, so he would not have to spend precious time cutting the padlock. The back entrance to the building was something else. The door was padlocked and bolted. For all Manuel knew, there was probably a silent alarm, which might go off at the local constabulary if it were tripped. He bade his troops stand quietly in an outer alcove, then signaled José and Rogelio to come with him as they searched the perimeter of the building.

He could not find any wires indicating an alarm system, but that didn't mean they weren't there. Halfway around the building Manuel found the main telephone line. He cut the line as a precaution, then continued circling the building. Still no sign of an alarm system. When the three men returned to where they'd started, they searched for the largest exposed window they could find. José kicked at the window. It didn't give. He started swinging at the window with his rifle, to no avail. Manuel looked at his watch. Six-thirty. Half an hour 'til daylight.

"Don't waste your strength, *amigo*," Manuel replied. He raised his rifle and fired six shots into the glass. The shots opened up enough of a hole so that by using a large two-by-four they found nearby, the men were able to punch a hole big enough for them to step through. By daybreak, all of the Hispanics were inside the Libertyville cotton works.

ಸಾಡ

At six-thirty, Roy Kemp sat bolt upright in bed. He looked over at the other bed, where his wife continued to sleep deeply and peacefully. He'd had a bad dream or something, an inkling that told him that everything was not as it should be. This was unsettling, because Roy

CHAPTER 8

was a pretty deep sleeper himself. Maybe it was the food he'd eaten at Ruby's last night, or maybe it was just age catching up with him. The Kemps lived a quarter mile from the cotton works. An early morning walk would do him some good. After all, he did feel a sense of loyalty to his job, and it couldn't hurt to make sure everything was all right. Besides, the rain had let up a little bit and it wouldn't be that uncomfortable a walk. He grabbed his outfit from the night before, went into the living room, dressed quietly, and left home, headed for the Libertyville cotton works.

9

"What the fuck? It's that fat old guy, the night watchman, and he's headed straight for the building," Rogelio said. He glanced nervously at the *lider*. "Lobo," he said, sweat breaking out on his forehead despite the chill in the building, "first the van *doesn't* show up and now this old fart *does*. This is becoming one gigantic clusterfuck. If that guy finds the window kicked in and notifies anyone, our ass is grass."

"Calm down, Rogelio. I'll take care of this. What did you say the owner's name was?"

"Moses Mendelssohn."

"Mendelssohn? Ah, like the composer. I will handle this fellow with dispatch. Perhaps it won't even be necessary to use force," Manuel said, donning a sport jacket he'd brought with him for just such a contingency. "What's the watchman's name?"

"I don't remember," Rogelio said.

"I do," José said. "It's Kemp. Roger or Rick, something like that."

Manuel headed toward the front of the building and intercepted the night watchman just as he got to the parking lot. "Mister Kemp?" he called out. "Good morning, sir. Mister Mendelssohn told me you were a very loyal employee, so I'm not surprised you came over early on a Saturday morning to make sure everything was all right."

CHAPTER 9

Roy Kemp was surprised to find someone coming out the front door. Even more surprised that this stranger knew his name. I don't believe we've met Mister … ah … Mister …?"

"Maximilian Bragado-Galba y Alcantar. Most people call me Max."

"You got sorta' an accent, but I can't place it. Are you a *spic* … I'm sorry, I mean a Mexican?"

"Not at all, Mister Kemp," Manuel replied smoothly, not even letting on that he knew exactly what the watchman meant by this racial slur. "You have a very good ear for accents. I'm actually from Madrid, Spain."

Kemp lit up at the compliment. In order to further impress this obviously cultured man, he continued, "I know all about Spain. Did you know that one of your people, Christopher Columbus, discovered America?"

"It's something I learned in school back in Madrid," Manuel said, choosing to ignore the provincialism of this bumpkin, who didn't even know that Columbus was an Italian who'd been employed by Ferdinand and Isabella to hunt booty and treasure. "You've been at the Libertyville cotton works a while, have you?"

"Thirty years. Say, I heard a rumor that Mister Mendelssohn's trying to sell out. You wouldn't be the feller that's interested in buying, are you?"

"As a matter of fact, I am. Mister Mendelssohn's lawyer left me the key last night and told me to make myself at home. I'm supposed to meet Mister Mendelssohn later this morning. Would you care to show me around the perimeter of the place?"

The guard looked suspiciously at Manuel. The perimeter was forty acres and included a large tract of woods where anything could happen. No matter how smooth and authoritative this man sounded, there was something not quite right about the situation. "No offense y'understand, but Mister Mendelssohn didn't say a word about any buyer to me. I imagine Mister Peebles, his next in command, would have said something."

"I understand your hesitation," Manuel said. "I'd feel the same way as you unless I heard it 'from the horse's mouth.' Perhaps I should call Mister Mendelssohn? Is there a pay phone nearby?"

"There's one down at Ruby's, but at seven on a Saturday morning I wouldn't want to take a chance on callin' him."

"You're probably right," Manuel said. "I've got a pot of coffee going inside. Would you care to join me?"

"Well, maybe I could …" He started toward the front door, then hesitated for a moment and glanced at his watch. "On the other hand, Marge'll be waking up soon. Maybe it's best I be goin'. When do you think you might be takin' over the plant?"

Manuel shrugged as he walked Kemp out toward the road. "I don't even know if we can put a deal together, Mister Kemp. I wonder if I could trouble you for a little bit of information?"

"Well …?"

"I don't want you to betray any confidence. Maybe I could walk you a couple of blocks toward your home? If we take over the company, we'll almost certainly need your services." He could see suspicion turn to mild elation as the man puffed himself up. *Who knows? He might even be helpful.* As the two men started walking toward town, Manuel continued, "Mister Kemp?"

"Why not call me Roy?"

"If you feel comfortable with that, Roy, then. I'd like to ask your advice."

"Shoot."

"My company imports oranges from many countries – Mexico, Brazil, Israel …"

"Israel? No kiddin'."

"No kidding. I'm wondering if you think there'd be a market for oranges in this area, and if, perhaps, we might be able to ship them to surrounding towns?"

"Gee, Mister ... Mister ..."

"Max."

"Gee, Mister, uh, Max. I never really gave it much thought. Ruby's serves a great glass of O.J. every morning. Importing oranges? I don't know, Mister ... Max. There's a helluva lot of oranges in Florida."

"What if we could bring them in cheaper?" Manuel asked in a confidential, 'us against the world' tone of voice.

"Well ... there's lotsa' folks in this town'd work for whatever they could get. Rumor is the cotton works ain't long for this world. It's the only employer left in Libertyville. I think we might be able to compete with the big boys in Florida. My home's just down the street a bit. Wanna' come in for some coffee, Max?"

"I'll pass for now, Roy. Please keep our little conversation under your hat. It might not be a good idea for this kind of thing to get out too quickly. If we don't buy the company, it would disappoint a lot of good people, wouldn't it?"

"You're right, ... Max. Could you give me a hint of when you might know if this deal is coming off?"

"Sure, Roy. Between us, we should have things ironed out by next Thursday. But again, other than Mister Mendelssohn, you're the only one in town who knows anything about this. I promise you'll be the first one other than Mister Mendelssohn to know."

෴

Manuel Cabrera hadn't even made it back to the Libertyville cotton works before Roy Kemp had left his house for the second time that morning and headed toward Ruby's.

ಯಌ

"You kill the sumbitch, *lider*?"

"Naww. When we parted, he was eating outta' my hand. The imported orange story was the bait and the promise he'd be the first to be hired was the hook he couldn't refuse."

"You think he'll really keep it a secret?"

"Hell, no. If I had to bet, I'd say he's probably on his way to the local gab center even as we speak."

"D'you think that could be dangerous?"

"Not as dangerous as killing him and trying to dispose of the body. I think the rumor of a takeover and the knowledge that there's somebody from the new company here over the weekend will keep people talking so much they won't come near the place."

ಯಌ

Something just didn't feel right. He'd said he would meet Moses Mendelssohn at the factory at ten-thirty. He knew what he was supposed to say. The worst that could happen was Mendelssohn would say no. Moses Mendelssohn was not a hail-fellow-well-met, but Augustus had never known him to be deliberately rude. At the very least, he might be able to get Mendelssohn to think about the proposition.

He was secretly hoping Mendelssohn would say no and queer the deal, just so that arrogant sonofabitch Walker would be taken down a peg or two. Hoping Mendelssohn would say no? Was he crazy? Bishop Walker had told him he'd be falling into a very deep pit if he didn't bring this off. How deep could the pit be? Letitia would learn about Sarah. His congregation, such as it was, would whisper behind his back. Would he really be lynched? The odds were he'd simply pack up Letitia and the kids and make a new start a thousand miles away, on a moment's notice, *before* the shit hit the fan. Sarah Coben was no fool. Much of what she had said made sense to him.

Augustus Caesar Coyle was certainly young enough to start over. He had a college degree and enough savings to get by for a month or so. Why was he worrying his heart out about losing a fourteen hundred dollar a month job? Letitia wouldn't leave him, even if she found out about Sarah. Even if she did leave him, how much alimony and child support would he have to pay? You couldn't get blood out of a turnip. So why did he feel such tension, such a premonition of danger?

"Something bothering you, darling?" Letitia said, making sure his coffee cup was filled and he had another plateful of sticky buns, the kind he loved.

"No … Yes, 'Tish, it is. I feel I'm such a failure. Here I am, forty-two and what have I got to show for it? What do *you* have? – and I promised you so much."

She stood behind him, gently kneading the tight muscles of his neck and back, quietly waiting for him to finish. "Augustus Caesar Coyle, you are my man, and you are anything but a failure. Maybe this town is failing you, but you sure haven't failed the town."

"The Bishop …"

"He's worse than the town, honey. The church sure hasn't shown any appreciation for all your efforts. I married you for better or worse. I've never regretted it for a moment. Are you sure you're cut out to be a small town preacher? I'd follow you to the ends of the earth."

"You mean if I asked you to pick up and leave?"

"Tomorrow, honey. Tonight if you're in a hurry." She laughed gently, but meaningfully. "As long as we're together, darling, how could we fail? How long is your meeting supposed to last?"

"Forty-five minutes, maybe an hour at most."

"So you'll be back in time for lunch?"

"Uh-huh."

"Let's make a date. I'll send the kids over to my mama. When you come home, I'll have a nice hot lunch ready for you, and then …" she squeezed him lovingly and gave him a look full of sensual promise. "We can talk about whatever comes up."

❧☙

"I'm getting really hungry, *Lider*," José said. "That sorry excuse for a cafeteria downstairs had some cold coffee and some stale sandwiches in the fridge. No word on the van?"

"That does present a problem," Cabrera said. "The rain seems to be letting up a little. You feel like going on a foraging trip?"

"There's a Piggly Wiggly in Henderson, but in this weather it's a four or five hour drive each way," Rogelio said.

"Downtown Libertyville is only a few blocks away," José added.

"Great idea, smartass," Rogelio said sarcastically. "Three dozen tacos, a dozen burritos, a dozen *flautas*, lots of extra chili sauce, and *chimichangas* for twelve. Man, that'll set this place up a helluva lot faster than that fat-fuck guard, who's probably shooting his mouth off even as we speak."

"Fuck you," José replied, his tone surly. The tension, exacerbated by his hunger and the fact that he was just plain tired, was getting to him.

Manuel Cabrera slammed the lid on their argument quickly. "*Silencio!*" he roared. "Lest you forget, we are the advance guard of the army that's going to take over this place. A place where we'll bring our women and children. A place where we'll finally be accepted because *we'll* do the accepting. No more scraping and begging and kissing the white man's ass. You guys know what it's like. You've seen how the *Norteamericos* have dealt with us 'fuckin' beaners' for the last twenty years. Are you all of a sudden such pussies you can't miss a meal or a siesta for the sake of the cause? You're thirsty? Find the nearest sink. You don't like stale sandwiches? Take a hammer and bust open the vending machine. There's cookies and candies and potato chips and Coca Cola, everything you need to fill up your chickenshit little tummies. By tomorrow morning, we'll have full control of this place, and you can even use some of the coins you take out of the vending machines to buy some real food up in Tomkinsville. Do I make myself clear?"

Cabrera's two lieutenants nodded desultorily.

"OK, each of you give orders to those under your command. Four hours' sleep for the first group. The best place is probably the cafeteria. The second shift will keep guns at the ready until they're replaced. I expect my lieutenants to show by example how an army is supposed to work, *comprende*?"

ဢﬤ

"I tell ya', Jarrod, there's something funny about that feller." Roy Kemp and his buddy were seated at the counter at Ruby's. "At first, I was excited when the guy told me about his plans for the old plant. But then I thought to myself, here's this Mexican – and I don't care what he *said* he was, he looked like a beaner to me – talkin' about importing oranges from Brazil and Israel. Israel, for Christ's sake! That's halfway around the world. I sure as hell can't see how they could get oranges here cheaper than transporting 'em from Florida, particularly when them Florida growers is paying their pickers coolie wages."

"Sounds suspicious to me, all right. Who in his right mind would wanna' buy it? Buncha' old machinery, building's probably got about ten times the gov'mint maximum of asbestos. A hunnert miles to the closest port, ten miles to the nearest highway."

"I got half a mind to call old man Mendelssohn and ask him about it."

"More coffee, honey," Jarrod called out to Adeline the waitress, who must have worked at Ruby's fifty years or more.

As the elderly waitress approached, she said, "S'cuse me for buttin' in, boys, but I been listenin' to you talkin'. Wouldn't it be better to ask Madison Peebles if he knows anything?"

"Naww," Kemp replied. "I say we go to the main man." He looked up at the wall clock. "A little after ten. Adeline, can you find me his number?"

"Prob'ly listed," the waitress said. She reached under the counter and pulled out a thin telephone directory, about the same size as a schoolchild's notebook. "Darn! This thing gets thinner every year. Karbaugh, Klassen …" She licked her index finder and turned the page. "Mabel's Hair Salon, Marion …"

"Christ A'mighty, Adeline, if you take much longer finding it, we're all gonna' be dead," he laughed.

"Here 'tis," the waitress said triumphantly. "Mendelssohn, Moses, 1871 Creekside Road … 478-5475."

"Can I borrow yer phone to call?"

"Suit yourself. It's a local call."

Roy Kemp looked up at the clock again. "Maybe I better wait a few minutes in case he's sleeping in late. Old people are like that." The waitress glared at him. "I didn't mean you, Adeline. Hell, you 'n me 'n Jarrod, we're all about the same age, and I was up walkin' before seven."

CHAPTER 9

He signaled his cup. "Fill it up with Java. As soon as I bolt this down, I'll call him."

※

At ten that morning, Moses Mendelssohn finished his breakfast, brushed his hair, slapped some cologne on his face, and brushed his teeth. Twenty minutes later, he walked out to the attached garage and got into his Chrysler.

At that moment, the telephone started ringing in the kitchen. He debated with himself whether to answer it. It would take an effort to get out of the car and go back into the house. Who'd possibly be calling him on a Saturday morning? Wouldn't be a relative. They never called unless it was a Sunday afternoon. Probably a wrong number. Whoever it was, they could leave a message on the answering machine. If the call was important enough, he'd return it when he got back. Besides, it would take five minutes just to go into the house, say hello, and hang up. He'd promised to meet Preacher Coyle at the factory at ten-thirty and it wouldn't be polite to keep the clergyman waiting.

Mendelssohn checked the gauge to make sure there was at least half a tank of gas in the car, an old Saturday habit. Satisfied, he backed the car out of the driveway, and started down the hill toward the factory.

※

"That's odd. No one home," Roy Kemp said to his two friends. "After thirty years, you'd think I knew that old guy's habits pretty well. He must have gotten up early to go a'visitin'. Well, it's not as if I didn't try to warn him."

10

The Reverend Augustus Coyle was waiting in the front parking lot when Mendelssohn's Chrysler pulled up next to his Honda Accord.

"Sorry I'm late, Reverend Gus," the old man said.

"No problem at all, Mister Mendelssohn. I've been waiting all of a minute-and-a-half. Not a lot of traffic on a wet Saturday morning. At least the rain's let up some. Windy, though."

"That it is. Well, we might as well go on up to the office," Moses said, nodding in the direction of the third floor.

"Sure you wouldn't like to take a little walk around the place first?" Coyle asked.

"I don't think so. I'd like to hear what you have to say."

ഌ⚭

"What the …?" Rogelio shook Manuel Cabrera by the shoulder.

"What is it, Rogelio?" Manuel had nodded off for a couple of moments, but came instantly awake.

"Two guys. The owner and the local *Negrón* preacher man. They're comin' straight for the front door. What're we supposed to do now?"

"Where are the troops, *amigo*?"

"Half of 'em are asleep in the second floor cafeteria. The others are scattered."

"Signal them to *quietly* disperse to where they won't be seen."

"No problem."

"Good." He looked out the window toward the two newcomers. "The *Padre's* probably hitting the old guy up for a donation."

As he heard the front door open, he continued *sotto voce*, "My guess is they'll go into the old man's office to talk. There's no need for us to introduce ourselves 'til they've gotten nice and comfy. There's another office two doors down and a large storage room adjacent to that office. I'll hole up in there and make my move in precisely twenty minutes. Let's make sure our watches say the same thing. Meet me in the old guy's office at eleven o'clock straight up. *Vamanos!*"

ഈരു

As they entered the building, except for the front entry light, which was slaved to a timer, the place was dark. It was cold because the radiator's boilers had been turned off Friday night. As they walked down the hall, their heels clicking on the slate floor, two mice scampered by in front of them.

"You feel like taking the elevator up to my office, Reverend?"

"We'd probably get a bit warmer if we walked up."

"Good idea." He opened up a nearby control box and pulled up a handle. "Might as well get some heat in the place. Have you had breakfast yet, Reverend?"

"I have."

"Me, too. Want to stop in the cafeteria and get a cup of hot coffee?"

"Your preference, Mister Mendelssohn."

On the floor immediately above them, José, who had heard the exchange, whispered, "They're going toward the cafeteria. What happens if …?"

"They'll meet our reception committee."

"I know. But the leader said …"

"Don't worry, they're headed away from us. With the wind going through this drafty old building, I doubt they'd hear us if we shouted."

Mendelssohn and Coyle had just about reached the cafeteria door when Moses mumbled, "I forgot this is Saturday. There's nobody in the cafeteria. If there's any coffee left in the urn, it's a day old and cold by now."

"That's OK, Mister Mendelssohn. Too much caffeine in the morning gets me pretty wired."

The two men retraced their steps and walked up the stairway to the third floor. On the way to Mendelssohn's office, they passed Madison Peebles' office. As they did so, there was a sudden loud clanking noise. Augustus Coyle tensed and involuntarily asked, "What's that?"

"Heater kicking in," Mendelssohn said. "It's old and noisy, but it still gets the job done."

Inside the storage room, Manuel Cabrera had likewise become unnerved by the unexpected noise. He leaped to his feet and aimed his rifle at the door.

"Are you sure we shouldn't go inside that office, just to make sure everything's okay?" Coyle said, his hand on the doorknob.

"Suit yourself, Reverend," Mendelssohn responded. "If you want, you can look in every room and every nook and cranny of this place. One thing I can tell you: after fifty years in this building, there's enough strange noises every day that you could spend years investigating them and all you'd get would be tired of chasing your tail."

"If you say so," Coyle said, turning from the door.

They continued down the hall and entered Mendelssohn's office, which was plain and unadorned. The room was twenty feet square. The window at the far side overlooked the front of the factory and had a good view of Libertyville Road. The desk adjacent to the window was heavy, old, and scarred from years of use. Mendelssohn's black leather executive chair was positioned between the desk and the window. Like the desk, it looked well-worn and well-used. There was a gray foam cushion strapped to the lower part of the backrest. Coyle had seen such devices in several offices. While they were by no means ergonomic, he'd been told they provided good support for a man's lower back.

There were two comfortable-looking armchairs in front of the desk. Like Mendelssohn's chair, the black leather was cracked from years of use. A matching couch sat by the side wall to his left. A tall planter decorated the end closest to Mendelssohn's desk, and a floor lamp filled the space at the other end of the sofa. Coyle noticed a wooden door at each wall adjacent to Mendelssohn's desk. "Storage room to the left, bathroom to the right," Mendelssohn said. "All the conveniences of home." He chuckled mirthlessly.

"Nice place," Coyle said politely.

"Nice *old* place," Mendelssohn echoed. "I can't say I won't miss it." He sat down in his executive chair and motioned his visitor to sit down anywhere he wanted. Coyle pulled one of the nearby armchairs closer to the desk and sat down.

"What did you mean when you just said 'I can't say I wouldn't miss the place'? Do you intend to slow down?"

"Did I say that? Must've been daydreaming, although at seventy next month I can't say it would be a bad age to retire."

Mendelssohn's statement gave Coyle the opening he needed, but the Reverend felt it would not be good manners to rush his Bishop's directive. He stood up, walked over to the wall above the sofa, where he saw a fading painting of a much younger, smiling Moses Mendelssohn and a small, dark, pretty woman in her mid-thirties, who stood next to Mendelssohn. He looked toward the older man.

"Leah and me, nineteen sixty-six. Banner year for the plant. We went down to Mobile and visited one of those artists who paints portraits from a favorite family photo. Levy had died by that time and we didn't want something that would remind us of him every day, but we didn't want anything that would reflect our sadness either. It's still one of my favorite pictures. You don't have to say it, Reverend Gus. The painting's fading. Leah already faded out of life, and I suppose I'm not far behind. You want some water, Reverend? There are two glasses in the bathroom. I can get you some."

"Thank you, yes, Mister Mendelssohn." When the older man returned, Coyle sat down in the armchair again.

"How's your church doing, son?" Mendelssohn asked kindly. "I imagine with the town slowin' down and people dyin' or movin' out your congregation gets smaller and smaller each year. Must be difficult to make ends meet."

"That it is, Mister Mendelssohn."

Moses opened a desk drawer and took out a large checkbook, the kind with a row of three large checks on every page. He set it in front of him and took a ballpoint pen from the cupful of them on his desk. "I can make this a very short visit, Reverend," he said. "I'm sure you've heard talk that the factory's not in the best of shape, but there are those who are a lot worse off, and if I can help in some small way …" He started to write out a check, but Reverend Coyle held up his right hand, palm out.

"No, Mister Mendelssohn. That's very generous of you, but it's not really necessary. Our little congregation is part of a much larger church, and we're provided for. That's not really the reason I asked to see you today."

"It's not?" The older man seemed genuinely surprised. "Excuse me a moment, Reverend," he said, rising. "But when you get to be my age, it seems you have to relieve yourself every other moment."

When he returned, he said, "Ahhh, that's much better – at least for a few minutes. OK, Reverend, what was it you wanted to talk to me about?"

∞○∞

"So your church wants to acquire this place for the greater glory of God?"

"That's about it, Mister Mendelssohn."

"And, of course, the greater glory and the monetary enhancement of the church?"

Moses noticed that Coyle's face became noticeably darker as the reverend blushed. "I won't deny that."

"Nothing to be ashamed of, Reverend Gus. That seems to be the way of the world. After all, they call America the land of opportunity. I suppose that means the opportunity to make as much money as you can. Time for me to go to the toilet again," he said, standing up. On his return, Mendelssohn said, "Did your church give you any instructions on how to deal with *my* financial needs?"

"Not really," Coyle stammered. "They thought it might be something for negotiation between us."

Mendelssohn spun his chair around and looked out the window. It had started raining in earnest again, and the sky was noticeably darker than it had been when they'd first come into the room. "That road's gonna' be a cesspool soon," he said. Turning back toward Coyle, he said, "Good faith negotiations, eh?"

"Yes, sir."

"Provided I recognize that your church is the *good faith*."

"I guess you could say that, sir." Mendelssohn noticed he was blushing again.

"You know, son, you might make a helluva good preacher, but you'd make an awful liar. I don't believe you've gotten anything more from your church than them sayin' 'Soften him up. Say anything you gotta' say. Promise anything you gotta' promise. We want that property.'"

Reverend Coyle looked down at the floor and said nothing. The two of them sat in silence for a few moments. When Coyle raised his eyes to look directly at the factory owner, he saw nothing but kindness and patience on the face of the other man.

"Well, Reverend, you've made your pitch, and I can certainly vouch to your church headquarters you've done the best you can. But I'll level with you. Maybe it's just been rumor up to now, but I'll speak to you man to man. What I mean to say is …"

Suddenly there was the loud crash of the door being kicked in. A light-skinned, dark-haired man of early middle age, his rifle raised, faced them both.

"Good morning, gentlemen," said the intruder. "Permit me to introduce myself. I am Maximilian Bragado-Galba y Alcantar. I must respectfully advise both of you that whatever plans either of you may have for this place have been canceled. You are now speaking with one of the new owners of this establishment. I invite you to remain seated and perhaps neither of you will get hurt. It will take some time and some discussions to determine exactly how we will effectuate the change and announce it to the world. Ah, I see two of my associates have entered the room," he said, nodding at José and Rogelio, who had just appeared, their rifles trained on Augustus Coyle and Moses Mendelssohn. Gentlemen, let us all be seated. Mister Mendelssohn, with your permission, I feel it would be better if I occupied your chair for the moment. Feel free to seat yourself in one of the armchairs or on the sofa," he nodded. "Ahh, that's better. Gentlemen, let us begin our chat."

11

"You think you can force an armed takeover of this place?" Coyle was the first to recover.

"No, *Negrón*," Manuel replied. "We already *have* taken over this place. I have twelve armed associates scattered throughout this building, the advance guard. By tomorrow night, a hundred more will be in place."

"You feel a hundred will be enough to hold the factory?" Moses asked sardonically. "Against what might be a thousand?"

"Ha!" Manuel barked a short, ironic laugh. "This whole town doesn't have a third that number. Do you honestly believe the state law enforcement officers will gather in huge numbers to save this toxic waste dump you call a factory? Face it, old man, your so-called factory has become a blight on your so-called town, and your town has become a needless and expensive corpse for this county and the entire state. Anyone with a shred of common sense would realize we're doing the county and the state a favor. Like my people have done for hundreds of years, we're only taking over a place nobody else wants."

"All it will take is one telephone call," Moses said.

"Go ahead, if that's what you want to do. Don't worry," Manuel said, putting the rifle down. "I won't even shoot you." As Mendelssohn fumbled with the phone in frustration Manuel said mildly, "Oh, did

I forget to tell you the lines out of here have been disconnected? Pity. In any event, now that we know we're all alone, shall we continue our little talk?"

Mendelssohn, who'd been through worse – much worse – in his life, was neither particularly frightened nor particularly cowed by these gunmen. "All right, we'll talk. But before we do, I suggest you tell me your real name. You're no more a Spaniard than I am."

"I prefer to remain Maximilian Bragado-Galba y Alcantar for the moment in the unlikely event there's trouble later on. My associates, by the way, are José and Rogelio. I think their first names are all you need to know."

"How long do you expect this 'small chat' to last, Mister Bragado?"

"That depends, Señor Mendelssohn," Cabrera said softly. "It could very well take the rest of your life."

Moses shuddered inside but kept a deliberately calm exterior. "What makes you say that?"

"You're not a stupid man, Mister Mendelssohn. My associates and I could have papers ready and prepared for your signature. The moment we release you, I have no doubt you'd claim the papers were signed under duress, and who's anyone going to believe, a white man, even if he's a Jew, or a stupid, lazy Mexican? You get the picture, I'm sure."

Moses thought about the intruder's words for several moments. He felt his bladder constricting, something it had done for the past fifteen years every time he got nervous. He stood up.

"Where do you think you're going?"

"I'm going to the bathroom."

"I think not."

"Then you'll have to shoot me right now."

Cabrera raised his rifle and aimed it at Moses Mendelssohn.

CHAPTER 11

"Go ahead. You think your *machismo* will go up a notch with your friends when they find you shot an old man because he had to pee?" Mendelssohn ignored the gun and started for the bathroom. "And if you think I'll try to escape out a third story window that's too small for me to get out of, even if I could, or if you think I'll try to slit my throat with a razor that's not in there, you're more than welcome to come into the bathroom with me." Mendelssohn closed the door.

Cabrera waited a minute, then banged sharply on the door with the butt of his rifle. "Hey! What's taking you so long in there?"

"You want to come in and have a look? Or maybe you've never heard of an enlarged prostate."

Another minute went by. Mendelssohn emerged from the room and sat down in the armchair again. "That's better."

"Let me ask you something, Señor Mendelssohn. You don't impress me as a stupid or foolhardy man. Why would you risk your life by disobeying and walking out on me?"

"Very simple, Mister Bragado," Moses answered. "I am, as you say, neither particularly brave nor particularly stupid, but the one thing I will never let happen to me is that I will soil my pants in public – at least not willingly. I will die first."

"Why?"

"Many, many years ago, when the Nazis came into my small village, they played a nasty little game. I was twenty at the time and I'll remember it 'til the day I die. One morning, about seven o'clock, they gathered every Jewish male in town who was over the age of twelve and herded us into a nearby schoolyard. They invited – ordered – everyone else in the village to stand outside the fence and watch. They pushed and bullied us into rows of twenty, one behind the other. Then they stood facing us with their machine guns. We just stood there on the blacktop, and they stood on the blacktop. After a while, it was only natural that the men needed to urinate, and one or two of them raised their hands to ask to go to the bathroom.

"'*Nicht wahr*,' the closest officer said.

"'But, sir,' one of the older men said. 'We cannot just stand here all day and simply soil our pants?'

"'You can do whatever you want. It makes no difference to me. But let me tell all of you, you are standing on precious Reich soil. It is only by the sufferance of the regional commandant that you *Juden* are given the privilege of standing on ground that is above the likes of your subhuman race. So you will stand until I tell you you need not stand any longer, and you may soil your pants any way you want. You may piss your pants or you may shit your pants, but I will tell you this. If so much as one drop of your piss or your fecal matter falls upon this precious Reich soil you will personally lick it up. Is that clear?'

"No one answered. 'I said, "*Is that clear?*"' the officer barked.

"When there was still no answer, he walked up to the nearest man and cracked a whip across his face. He repeated, in much softer, but far more menacing tones, 'Is that clear, scum?'

"'*Jawohl, Herr Offizier!*' we called out as loud as we could.

"That day, the Nazis kept us standing until long after the sun went down – and that was after eight at night. The Poles, our neighbors, who were looking at us from outside the yard, thought this was a marvelous spectator sport. They jeered at us throughout the day, and they were usually quicker than the Nazis to spot when a drop of moisture 'polluted' the precious Reich soil. Many of the men couldn't hold it in. As they were licking up their waste, the Nazi guards kicked at them and struck them with quirts or brooms, or the butt-handles of their guns, whichever was nearest to hand. Ten Jews died that day. Ten out of a hundred, Mister Bragado. Ten percent of the Jewish population of Fajsławice. Every one was someone's grandfather, father, brother, husband, it didn't matter. As far as the Master Race was concerned, for every one that died there was one less piece of subhuman scum to inhabit their *lebensraum*.

"Mister Bragado, I was one of the only ones who held it in all day. I never forgot the way I felt when I was allowed to return home that night. Does that answer your question?"

"It does, Señor Mendelssohn. I truly regret I had to make you relive that moment, but it was a necessary question."

"I don't take offense, Mister Bragado. You are doing what you feel you have to do, and I just did what I had to do." Mendelssohn took a deep breath and exhaled before he continued. "Will you answer me a question now?"

"Yes, Señor."

"Why are you doing this?" He spread his hands out to indicate the property. "What good does this do you? What do you have to gain? This is one of the poorest forty acres in the poorest town in one of the most depressed areas of the United States."

"Señor Mendelssohn, I am well aware of that. It is also wealthier than ninety percent of all the land in Mexico."

"But many of your people already live on this side of the border," Augustus Coyle interjected.

"For the time being. Of course, who knows how long that will continue? Even if they can't get rid of us, everywhere we go we are spat upon, laughed at, third class citizens. Of those Mexicanos who live in the *Estados Unidos*, did you ever stop to think how many of them live ten to a room? Or how many are cheated out of their wages by their *gringo* bosses? Or how many have their identities checked five times a day? Every time a white man looks at one of us, he is thinking, 'That's probably an illegal who's taking away *my* job, *my* source of a living, *my* paycheck.'

"And yet when it comes to the work nobody wants to do – not even the *Negroes* – who are the first ones to be called on? Who cleans out the sewers of the wonderful American cities? Who are the maids and the gardeners and the ones who go out in the fields with their short-handled hoes and break their backs and their spirits so that the *gringos* can buy lettuce for less than a dollar a head?" Cabrera shook his head in bitterness.

"You're not telling me anything I don't know," Augustus rejoined. "We've been there for almost four hundred years."

"Yes, *Negro*," the other said. "But the operative word is *been* – past tense. "If your people are suspected of anything, they may do time in the county jail or even state prison, but they're not packed up and shipped back to another country, wife, kids, and all. They don't put up barbed wire fences and station armed guards at the borders to keep you from traveling to or living in another state. Regardless of how bad you act, you are looked on as *Americans*. How many Japanese do you see the authorities sending back? How many Koreans? How many Vietnamese? None. They all get to stay here, never mind how they got here. But we Mexicans? We are the forgotten ones, the ones nobody talks about, as if, God forbid, what we have may be *catching*."

"You still haven't answered my question," Moses Mendelssohn said quietly. "Why are you doing this? What good does this do you? What have you got to gain?"

"Everyone wants land of their own, a place to go to that's home. A place where no one can bully you or say you don't belong, where you live at the sufferance of others. Have you ever traveled to the Holy Land – to Israel, Mister Mendelssohn?"

"Twice, once in nineteen-sixty and again in nineteen-ninety-one."

"Have you ever visited the West Bank?"

"Yes."

"So have I, Mister Mendelssohn. Have you ever seen a more wretched place in your life? Limestone *karst*, the famous Jordan River, which is twenty feet across at its widest, a countryside that makes Mexico look like an earthly paradise. The most meaningless piece of rock in the world, yet thousands of Palestinians are willing to become suicide bombers, to kill other human beings for no reason other than that they want that place for their own."

"You said Mexico looks like an earthly paradise."

"Oh, yes," Cabrera said. "There are many places where it is just that. But my people have never learned to work together. It's one for *one* and one for *one* again. My brother Hugo saves every penny he makes working as a laborer in El Paso, where he is shunned and shamed each day of his life. Three years ago, he took everything he had saved, ten thousand American dollars, into Mexico to give to his family in Oaxaca. Ten thousand dollars. You may as well come to Mexico with a million dollars. Fifty miles south of Ciudad Juarez, he was waylaid, attacked by four *Mexican* citizens in broad daylight. They tore apart his car to find that money, made him undress at gunpoint, and when they could only find eight thousand dollars, they shot him in both legs and left him naked and stranded ten miles from the nearest town of any size. That was *his* people, not a case of Germans and Poles and Jews fighting one another. Last year, almost the same thing happened. It was only a miracle that the *Federales* stopped the *bandidos* in time, and then *they* extracted five thousand dollars from Hugo before they let him go. So you see, Mexico is simply not a place for the average Mexican. It is if you are very rich and very powerful, but there is more poverty in Mexico every day.

"So where do we go? The only answer is for us to establish our own outposts, our own small towns, preferably small enough and indistinct enough so that we manage somehow to blend into the countryside, in the U.S.A."

"You hardly sound like the stereotype Mexican."

"I trust you've never met a cultured, educated *Mexican*, which is why I've managed, to a greater or lesser extent, to pass as a Spaniard."

"Where did you go to school, Mister Bragado?"

"The University of Mexico in Mexico City," he said. "Then I took a J.D. from Southwestern University Law School in Los Angeles."

Now it was Moses Mendelssohn's turn to stand and stretch. "Mister Bragado, you interrupted Reverend Coyle and me at a very good – or very bad – time. I trust you heard the last ten minutes of our conversation?"

"I did. The preacher's church wants the same land we want for their own purposes."

"That's true. But you interrupted us just at the moment when I was starting to tell him the property isn't available."

"Ah," said Manuel. "If it isn't available to the church then there is room for you and me to talk."

"No, Mister Bragado. It's not available to your people either. Late last week I concluded a deal with a very large company in Atlanta. I signed on the dotted line, which means I gave my word. Escrow opened three days ago. In twenty-seven more days the entire property will belong to the new owners. As a matter of fact," he looked at his watch, "their representative should be here within the next hour-and-forty minutes for an inspection tour of the place."

12

Terry Prince, the Coast Conglomerates representative, had taken Delta Flight 201 out of Atlanta at ten that morning for the one hour eleven minute flight to Mobile. The plane landed fifteen minutes late, at ten-thirty Mobile time. At quarter to eleven, he'd telephoned Moses Mendelssohn's home. No one answered. Half an hour later, Prince had called the Libertyville cotton works and gotten a continuous busy signal for fifteen minutes. At noon, he pulled into a Holiday Inn parking lot. One thing you could count on with Holiday Inn: if there was a restaurant on the premises, they always served a decent lunch.

Just after lunch, he telephoned Moses Mendelssohn's home again. Still no answer. He was making good time he'd probably arrive by two-thirty. He dialed the factory again. Still a busy signal. Then he telephoned his boss in Atlanta and reported in. "Have you heard any word from Mendelssohn at your end?" he asked his superior.

"Nothing here, Terry. I'm sure he would have called if it was off. I guess you'll just have to drive to the factory. You know how to get there?"

"Affirmative."

Letitia Coyle glanced nervously at the kitchen clock. One-fifteen. Augustus had said he'd be home before noon. She'd taken the kids over to her mother, showered, and donned her sexiest outfit – shorts and a halter top – despite the chill rain outside. She'd make sure he had a light lunch and then she expected things would get *very* warm. Although she hadn't told Augustus, for the past month she'd been surfing the net to find new places where they might live. Although her parents both lived in Libertyville, she had no love for the small town where she'd grown up. She thought she'd left the town behind once and for all when she'd graduated Valley State College two hundred miles to the north, but when she'd married Augustus Coyle, they'd somehow ended up back in this mud puddle of a town.

She'd finally came up with what she thought was the perfect place, San Diego, California. From all accounts, it was African-American-friendly, had a healthy economy, and a number of African-American churches. The large Mexican population might not be a good thing, but she could live with it.One-twenty. It was not like Augustus not to call. Maybe that horse's ass of a bishop, William Wyatt Walker – "Whine, Whip, and Whore" she secretly called him – had made good on his threat to come down to Libertyville. If that happened, she knew Augustus would be trapped in meetings until late into the night. Damn! Augustus was such a good man. Why was he ruining his life as a slave to "the Man," as she called the church? The church hadn't done a damned thing for him and she could see his life, his spirit, oozing away, a little more each month.

She glanced appreciatively at herself in the full-length bedroom mirror. "Man, for a thirty-five year-old gal with two kids, you are one good-looking woman!" she said, proudly lifting her breasts with her hands. "That preacher man's gonna' have all he can handle if he gets here soon enough."

One-thirty. Still no Augustus. Still no call, not even from the bishop. She was getting nervous.

෨෬

"It's certainly not like my uncle not to answer his phone on a Saturday," Sarah said, perplexed.

"Maybe he's gotten some of that old-time religion and decided he's not going to do any work, not even to lift up a telephone, on *Shabbos*."

"Not bloody likely, Mordechai. Something's wrong. I feel it. Have you ever had a premonition that something hasn't happened yet, but it's about to?"

"Once, Sarah."

"Sylvia?

"Uh-huh."

"Mordechai, I know it's *Shabbos* and all, and you're not permitted to drive or do work of any kind. But does God make an exception if there's an emergency?"

"Of course. On *Yom Kippur*, the Day of Atonement, when all Jews are supposed to fast, a man is directed to suspend that fast to take medication."

"I didn't say my uncle is sick. It's just a premonition and probably a silly one at that."

"Sarah, I've learned not to laugh at premonitions."

"In this weather, it'll take three-and-a-half hours to get to Libertyville. I hate to act like a simpering woman, but I don't feel comfortable making that drive alone, particularly after it gets dark. There's no other friend I could ask…"

"Well, it's one heck of a distance to go for a premonition, but I can't say I wouldn't enjoy the company. One caveat, though."

"Yes?"

"This may sound hypocritical to you, but if I go along, would you mind driving – at least until sundown? After all, this is your premonition, not mine. You may be exempt from the strict observance of the Sabbath, but I'm not."

※

Bishop William Wyatt Walker checked his Rolex. One-thirty. You'd think Brother Coyle would have had the decency to call by now. There must have been some kind of indication from the old Jew, one way or the other. He'd told his subordinate that he might be going down to Libertyville. The weather had not gotten any better, but the church had a helicopter on the roof, and the pilot could probably have him down to Libertyville in a little over an hour.

He reached for his desk phone and punched in a series of numbers. When the party at the other end picked up the phone, he was all oily sweetness. "Letitia, my dear, how good to hear your voice. Is our brilliant young pastor there, by any chance? Hmmm. You don't say. You've not heard from him? Yes, my dear, that is a bit odd. Not to worry, I just wanted to tell him I'll be flying down and I expect to be in your fair hamlet within the hour. No, you needn't come into town to pick me up. I'll be in the church's whirlybird and we can land inside the parking lot. Thank you, my dear. I'll talk to you later."

※

Roy Kemp had just placed a quart of milk, a loaf of Wonder Bread, a package of Oscar Mayer wieners, and a six pack of Bud on the checkstand conveyor belt when he saw Madison Peebles come through the door. "Hey, Mister Peebles!" he called.

"Afternoon, Roy."

"Could I speak with you for a few minutes when you're done, Mister Peebles?" the watchman asked. "Maybe we could stop at Ruby's for a cup of coffee and some apple pie?"

CHAPTER 12

"You sure you want to be seen with an old black man like me?"

"Hell, yes, Mister Peebles. This is the late twentieth century. People aren't like that no more."

"People don't change, Mister Kemp. Especially not in the South. Or haven't you noticed the Confederate flags that go up on certain days each year? Looks like you're done shoppin' and I'm not in any hurry. It's only a couple doors away."

The two men went into the coffee shop. Adeline greeted them. "Lord ha' mercy, I get t'see Roy Kemp twice in one day. And y'all got your boss man with you. Howdy-hi, Mister Peebles. As you can see, there ain't nobody here, so you got the whole place to yourselves. Sit anywhere you want. You get a'hold of Mister Mendelssohn yet, Roy?"

"No'm."

"Well, you got the Number Two man, so you can prob'ly find out what you need to find out."

"Much obliged, Adeline," Kemp said. He led Peebles to the back of the restaurant and they sat down in one of the plastic-covered booths.

"Mister Peebles, I don't mean to come right out and say it, but have you heard anything about Mister Mendelssohn selling out the cotton works?"

Peebles hesitated. He knew rumors were all over town, but he had no idea how much the night watchman knew. "Well, I cain't say that I have an' I cain't say that I haven't," he replied cautiously. "Do you know something I don't?"

Now it was the watchman's turn to be cagey. "The word's gettin' out more and more, and I know that you and Mendelssohn are as tight as two cats in a bag." He watched himself, lest he said the more common, "*Coons* in a bag." "I think maybe I mighta' met one of the buyers, if there was such a thing – and I know enough to keep it to m'self. I said *if* there was such a thing, y'understand."

Mendelssohn had told Madison Peebles the buyer's rep would be coming in this afternoon. In fact, Peebles had planned to sashay on over to the factory at about four, to meet the new fellow. Now it seemed he might have been pre-empted.

"What kinda' fella'd you meet?" Madison asked.

"Tall, light-skinned, dark-haired guy about forty or so. A foreigner. Said his name was Max Bragado-something, and he was from Spain."

"You said you can keep a confidence, Roy Kemp. Can you really?"

"Swear on my wife's corset." He winked and laughed coarsely. "Or anything else you might want," he said, more seriously.

"Okay. You been on the payroll thirty years. I s'pose you can keep your trap shut as well as anyone. Mister Mendelssohn told me earlier in the week he'd sold out the factory. He told me that someone who represents the buyer was going to come in today to inspect the place. That's about all I know. Don't know the buyer's name, don't know what he looks like, don't know anything about him. Y'say you met him earlier?"

"Yeah, seven o'clock this mornin'. Adeline, I'll have a slice of apple pie and coffee. How about you, Mister Peebles?"

"The same."

"Make that two, honey," Kemp called to the waitress. He turned back toward Peebles.

"What was the guy like?"

"Hard to say. Seemed pretty smooth, but there was something – I can't put my finger on it – that I didn't trust about the guy. I tried to call Mister Mendelssohn earlier today, but I couldn't get him at home. He could've gone out of town, although with this weather I don't know why he'd want to."

CHAPTER 12

That struck Madison Peebles as odd. Mister Mendelssohn had distinctly told him he'd be meeting with the new buyer's agent today, and he'd specifically invited Madison to come by and meet the guy in the afternoon. Moses Mendelssohn was not the kind to jump out of bed on a Saturday, so it would seem he should have been home in the late morning, unless, of course, he'd gone down to the factory to clean things up. "Did you try calling the factory?"

"Naww. I didn't think to do that."

"I'm sure there's an explanation. I'd heard the buyer was coming in this afternoon, but I may have been mistaken. Man, I forgot just how good the apple pie at Ruby's can be," he said, forking some of the delicious pastry into his mouth. "You know, they always make it too sweet in the supermarket."

"Yeah, I suppose," Kemp replied. "Do you think maybe we should go over to the factory, just to check that everything's on the up and up?"

"Cain't hurt," the black man said. "Mister Mendelssohn wanted me to meet the new guy anyway." He looked at his watch. "Two forty-five. I suppose if we mosey on over there about four-thirty, that should give everybody enough time to meet each other and have a good chat."

§)Q3

By three that afternoon, the Mexicans were, to a man, hungry, thirsty, and exhausted. They'd had nothing to eat for more than eighteen hours. The last of the stale sandwiches, potato chips, snacks, and drinks had been exhausted by noon, and there had been only enough to parcel out what was left to five of the men, including José and Rogelio. That left nine men without any sustenance. The mood among the twelve foot soldiers was surly.

Upstairs, in Moses Mendelssohn's office, the flood of talk had slowed to a trickle. Moses was old and he was tired. For the past several years, he'd taken naps on weekend afternoons. Fear might be one thing, but it did not stop him from nodding off.

Reverend Coyle was significantly more frightened than Mendelssohn. There had never been good blood between Hispanic-Americans and African-Americans, since both of those oppressed and weak minorities had engaged in what the downtrodden have done for thousands of years in every society. Too weak numerically and financially to take on the power-wielding majority, they fought one another over the table scraps that "the Man" stingily doled out to them. Society's losers, who'd historically represented ten percent of the population, fought bitterly, often to the death, over five percent of the nation's wealth.

Augustus saw the present situation as a replication of what had gone on for years. He was painfully aware that the Hispanics were on the ascendant in this country. He'd read where they accounted for almost half of the people in California, America's most populous state. They'd also made substantial inroads throughout the southwest, in Texas, and in Florida. Reverend Coyle knew that the Worldwide Church of Christ controlled more money than the Mexicans – for the time being. But it was a classic battle. A battle over a piece of real estate so poor they were the *only* ones who wanted it. *Well*, he thought, *that's not quite true. "The Man" wants this property for some reason, but just like us, they smell money, and more money.*

As if to underscore his thoughts, at that moment a new Buick pulled into the parking lot and a short, natty white man emerged from the driver's door. José was the first of the Hispanics to see him. He touched Manuel on his shoulder and pointed out the window. "More company, *lider*," he said. "Maybe he brought some food with him."

There was humorless laughter among the three Mexicans. "Is that the guy from the company?" he asked the soporific Mendelssohn.

CHAPTER 12

"Huh?" the old man said, waking up and looking out the window. "I guess so. I've never met the guy before."

"Well, you'd better go downstairs and greet him, *gringo*," Manuel said. "And no funny business. José and Rogelio will be on either side of the hall, just out of sight. They'll have their guns up and ready, and they'll know in an instant if there is. You understand?"

"I do."

"Good. Bring him up to your office – take the stairs, don't take the elevator. When he gets here, we'll be part of the welcoming committee."

13

"You think you can get away with this?" An outraged Terry Prince directed his venom directly at Manuel Cabrera. "Coast Conglomerates employs fifty-five thousand people in seventeen countries around the world. You've got a hundred man army? Let's say on your best day you can muster four or five hundred, although I doubt you have anywhere near that number. The courts will easily uphold the contract. Even Mister Mendelssohn will testify on our behalf."

"The way of the world, eh, Señor Prince. The big company will beat the little guy into submission ten times out of ten," Cabrera said.

"That's right," Prince replied. "Ten out of ten."

"A hundred out of a hundred?" Cabrera said, smiling.

"You got that right."

"But you only have one life, *amigo*. And face it, as far as you're concerned, that's the only life that counts. So your company may well win a hundred cases out of a hundred in the courts, but today the odds are fifteen to three in our favor, and we hold the power of life and death over the three of you. A courtroom victory won't do you a damned bit of good if you aren't around to enjoy it."

"I …" Prince spluttered.

"I think you've talked enough for awhile, Mister Prince. "Maybe it's time I did some of the talking."

CHAPTER 13

Prince glared at Manuel, but said nothing.

"I'll accept your representation that Coast Conglomerates has a valid contract with Moses Mendelssohn. Thus, in thirty days' time, as soon as escrow closes, Coast is the legitimate owner of the Libertyville cotton works and the forty acres surrounding it. Are we on the same page so far?"

"Go ahead," Prince said, tightly.

"You've heard the term 'double escrow,' Mister Prince? That's something American businesses do all the time. It means Coast has bought the *right* to purchase Libertyville cotton works, even though *delivery* only takes place on close of escrow. Meanwhile, Coast has the absolute *legal* right to sell its right to purchase the factory during escrow, correct?"

"It seems you know something about the law," Prince grudgingly admitted.

"Thank you, Señor Prince. As a matter of fact, I'm admitted to the bars in both California and Texas."

"Very well, Mister …?"

"Bragado will do for our purposes." Cabrera heard a shuffling noise and some shouting downstairs. "Rogelio," he said, turning to one of his two subordinates. "Find out what's going on down there and put an immediate stop to it, okay?"

Rogelio nodded and left the room. Cabrera resumed. "What is your position with Coast Conglomerates, sir?"

Throughout this interchange, Moses Mendelssohn was fast asleep, and now he had started snoring loudly. Augustus Coyle stood up and indicated he wanted to go to the bathroom.

"You got the same problems as the old man?" José asked, sneering.

"No," Augustus replied, "but we've been here since ten-thirty and it's now almost quarter of four. More than five hours. You may have an iron bladder, but I don't."

"OK, *Negrón*, we'll make it one on one. We go into the bathroom together. You piss, then you come out and I piss. Only when I do it, the door is open, just in case there's any funny business. They say *Negroes* are hung like horses. I can promise you this, *Negrón padre*, you try anything, anything at all, it won't make any difference if it's six inches or six feet. One little bullet from this rifle will cut it down to size, *comprende*?"

At that moment, a rifle blast exploded downstairs. The five men in Mendelssohn's office froze. The first to recover was Manuel Cabrera, who nodded to José to keep everyone covered, then wtalked o the far door. He was just about to call out, "What was that?" when an obviously shaken Rogelio came up the stairs.

"What happened?" Manuel asked coldly.

"There was a fight, *lider*. Two men on two men. I yelled at them to stop immediately. They completely ignored me. I shouted again, louder this time, and the ringleader told me to fuck off. Then he accidentally walked into a bullet, just as I was about to aim my rifle toward the ceiling. I don't think he'll be a ringleader anymore."

"You killed him?"

"No, *Lider*, as I said before, he *accidentally* walked into a bullet that just *happened* to go off in his direction."

"Shit, Rogelio!" Manuel stormed. "Do you realize we could have a revolt on our hands – a revolt coming from *our* people? One thing's for damned sure. You'd better watch your own ass from now on, 'cause you damn well fuckin' better believe they're gonna' be out for your ass, and your *cojones*, and every other part of you."

CHAPTER 13

"But, *Lobo* ..."

"No excuses, asshole!" Manuel was getting angrier by the moment. All eyes in Mendelssohn's office, including Moses', were on the ugly scene being played out.

"All right, Rogelio. Tell me just how you're going to handle this from here on out. These guys, the *soldados*, the foot soldiers, the *enlisted* men, look at us as their officers, their leaders. There are three of us and eleven of them, all armed. You killed one of *theirs*, *amigo*. Now it's not all fifteen of us against the *Negrón* and the *gringos* anymore. It's *them* against *us*. We've got a three-way standoff. We've got Mendelssohn, the reverend, and the guy from Coast as prisoners. But now *we're* prisoners as well. We're in no position to go downstairs and confront them."

Manuel Cabrera was silent for a moment, thinking. He looked directly at Reverend Coyle and José. "Gentlemen," he said in a calm, more rational voice. "I believe you said you had to relieve yourselves before much longer. Go ahead and do it."

When they returned, Manuel said, "All right, anyone else have to go?" Mendelssohn and Prince relieved themselves in turn. "José, Rogelio, keep an eye on these men. I can think more clearly if I relieve myself as well."

"Rogelio," he said, when he emerged, "I think maybe it's a good idea if you and I go downstairs together and do what we can to make peace with the men."

"But *líder*, you said it was up to us to maintain control."

"It is, but the officers must also keep the respect of their troops. When an officer can admit to a mistake, that may restore their confidence. *Andalé, amigo.* Let's go and get it over with."

ೞთ

"Gentlemen, *muchachos*," Manuel Cabrera addressed eleven surly men. " I accept full responsibility for what happened. For me to say I am sorry is not good enough. It will not bring Salvador Carillo back to life."

There was angry grumbling. "You got that right, *lider*," a voice from the crowd erupted. "So what do you intend to do?"

"I intend to make it up to you," Manuel said. "Señor Torres, do you have a few words to say?"

Rogelio, trembling, faced the enraged mob. "It was … it was an accident, my friends. We have been *compadres* since we all started together, you know it was …" He stopped in mid-sentence. Manuel had drawn a small handgun from a holster at his side. Without so much as a sidewise glance, he brought the pistol up while Rogelio was talking and dispatched him with a single clean shot to the head.

"Now, *Hermosos*," Manuel said smoothly. "We are even and we are back to where we were. Hernán," he said, addressing one of the group, "I will now need someone to replace our fallen comrade. Please come with me. As for the rest of you, I know you are hungry and I know you are tired. As soon as the day ends, I promise you on my honor I will dispatch three of you to go and bring back some food. Meanwhile, my *bravos*, have courage. We have a new world to win, and you are the forefront of our forces. I'm sure each of you will behave like the lion you are." He reached over to where Rogelio had fallen, seized his rifle, and handed it to the surprised Hernán. "Come, *amigo*. I need your help upstairs."

As Manuel and Hernán got to the top of the stairs, they suddenly heard a loud *whop-whop-whop-whop-whop* noise, as a large black, red, and white helicopter landed at the far end of the Libertyville cotton works' parking lot.

"What the …?" gasped José

CHAPTER 13

As the large rotor slowed to a whine, a tall, portly Black man in late middle age emerged, wearing multicolored vestments. A huge wooden cross depended from his neck. "Oh, my God," Augustus Coyle gasped. "It's Bishop Walker."

14

No one greeted the bishop. He rang the bell and banged on the door, but to no avail. From outside, the factory looked deserted. "Brother Coyle!" Bishop Walker called out loudly. "I know you're in there. Come down and let me in this instant!"

There was no response from within. The bishop looked toward the parking lot. Three cars, one of which he recognized as Reverend Coyle's Honda, and the church helicopter sat as silent sentinels. He signaled his pilot. "Brother Luke, I sense something is amiss here. The place looks deserted but it obviously is not. Brother Coyle's conveyance and two others are parked in yonder lot. Unless there was a fourth vehicle or unless they've all taken a rather long walk – both of which possibilities I strongly doubt – there must be people inside. I wish you to assist me in breaking down this door. After you do, just on the supposition that Brother Coyle and I might be in some danger, I'd like you to fly up to Tomkinsville. There's a state patrol office there. They might be of assistance."

"Wouldn't it be more prudent for me to radio them and we sit safely in the helicopter until they arrive, Excellency?"

The bishop thought for a brief moment. "You're right, Brother Luke. If Brother Coyle has placed himself in harm's way, there's no sense in either of us casting ourselves in the same danger. Besides, it appears the rain is starting once again."

☙❧

"What's he doing?" Manuel asked José.

"He and the pilot came to the front door. They stood there talking for a little while. Then they returned to the chopper."

"I wouldn't be surprised if they're trying to raise the state patrol," Cabrera said. "That's the last thing we need."

"Why not let me go out and talk to him? Perhaps bring him inside?" Augustus spoke up.

"You're asking me to trust you, *Negrón*?" Manuel asked. Give me one reason why I should?"

"I'll give you three good reasons, Mister Bragado. Two of them are sitting right over there," he said, pointing to Terry Prince and Moses Mendelssohn. I trust you'd be cautious enough to have a gun trained on me from the minute I left this office until the time I returned."

"True, *Padre*, but I can't read lips at a distance of one foot, let alone a hundred yards. You've got to come up with something better. If you don't, once they contact the state patrol we've got nothing to lose by taking out all three of you."

"How about this?" It was Terry Prince who, until that moment, had maintained his silence. "Send your lieutenant out with Reverend Coyle. He can make up any story he wants. I'm sure word has gotten around town that *someone* is planning to buy up the Libertyville cotton works, only no one knows who it is. Your second in command can masquerade as the buyer's representative."

"Not a bad idea, Coast Conglomerates man. Why are you on our side all of a sudden?"

"Don't fool yourself, Mister Bragado. If I thought I could get away with it, I'd be the first one to turn you in to the authorities. But, as you very adroitly put it, my odds aren't very good at this moment."

Manuel considered the situation. He looked directly at José. "What do you say *amigo*? You think you and Hernán can handle Señor Mendelssohn and Señor Prince if the Reverend and I go out and speak with the bishop?"

"I think that's a good idea. Hernán and me plus two guns to none are certainly enough to handle these two."

❦

"I can't raise the state patrol, Bishop Walker," Luke said apologetically. "Must be an antenna down between here and Tomkinsville. I could fly up there."

"That won't be necessary Brother Luke. Look yonder. As I live and breathe, it's Brother Coyle and he's with another man, not Mendelssohn. Mayhap it's Mendelssohn's lawyer?"

The helicopter continued to sit in silence, a large, ungainly-looking, sleeping bird. Bishop Walker emerged in full panoply and approached the two men.

"Brother Coyle," he said mock-sternly. "Did you not hear me knocking?"

"Unfortunately not, Excellency," Coyle said, bowing to the older man. "Mister Bragado and I were engaged in serious conversation. I'm afraid I didn't hear you."

"Surely you saw the helicopter?"

"No, Excellency, we were at the rear of the building and there are no windows looking out onto the parking lot from there. Your Excellency, may I present ..."

"Maximilian Bragado-Galba y Alcantar, Your Grace," Manuel said, elevating the proud bishop at least one step higher than he was. "Am I to understand you are a Cardinal in the Worldwide Church of Christ? I am deeply honored," Manuel said, bowing and actually kissing the ring on the bishop's extended hand.

"My, my," the bishop said, delighted both at the elevation of his rank and the humility of this obviously cultured man.

"Señor Alcantar, you are from ...?"

"Madrid Spain, Your Grace. I represent the purchaser of the Libertyville cotton works ..."

"The purchaser?" Bishop Walker said, somewhat aghast.

"Yes. However, your Reverend Coyle and I have been talking for several hours about the needs and desires of the church. I believe we may be able to come to an accommodation."

"Ah, yes?" The bishop preened, mightily pleased. "I am sure you and the Reverend Coyle have had a most ... productive afternoon. If I may be so bold to ask, Señor Alcantar, do you occupy a position of influence with your principal?"

"I am corporate senior vice president in charge of mergers and acquisitions, Your Grace."

"Would it be stepping beyond my bounds to ask if you are vested with authority to, as you say, come to accommodation with the church?"

"Not at all, Your Grace. I assure you I have full warrant to do so."

The bishop reached into the pocket of his capacious gabardine and brought out two large Havana cigars. "Do you smoke, Señor Alcantar? I'm told many of your countrymen do."

"Indeed," Manuel said. He reached out and took one of the proffered cigars, ran it lightly under his nose, sighed, and said, "Ah, Your Grace, you have exquisite taste. *Montecristo A Gran Corona*."

"And you, Señor Alcantar are obviously a highly cultured and worldly-wise man. Perhaps you and I can finish the, er, arrangements. I'm certain if we can come to a mutually satisfactory resolution, it should be between parties of equal standing, wouldn't you say?"

What an arrogant, self-aggrandizing bastard, Manuel thought. *It will be such a pleasure to take him down to where he belongs.* He smiled his most ingratiating smile, displaying white, even teeth, and said, "Your Grace, perhaps we might adjourn to the executive offices inside. Mister Mendelssohn may join us. He's given his blessing, in principle of course, but, as I'm sure you surmise, he's an elderly gentleman and has become exhausted by the day's events. Would your pilot care to join us? There are ample comestibles in our commissary, and I'm certain he'd be more comfortable inside."

The four men, all in seeming high spirits and good humor, entered the building together. "If you don't mind, sir," Manuel said to the pilot, "Cardinal Walker, Brother Coyle, and I will take the elevator to the third floor. The commissary is on the second floor, halfway down the hall on the right. I'm certain you'll be able to find your way there with ease. Unless, of course, you'd prefer to accompany the three of us to Mister Mendelssohn's executive suite?"

"No, sir," the pilot grinned. "I'd just as soon leave you high-and-mighties to your own business. Is there anyone in the commissary this late on a Saturday afternoon?"

"Of course," Manuel said smoothly. "Since you'll be the only customer at this time of day, I'm sure the personnel you find will swarm all over you and cater to your every wish."

☙❧

CHAPTER 14

"Exactly what kind of trick is this? What in the world do you think you're doing, Mister Alcantar?" the bishop said, giving voice to the shock and outrage he felt churning inside him when he'd entered Mendelssohn's office to be met with two raised guns. He glared at the erstwhile friendly Spaniard and found himself looking down the barrel of a third gun, a rifle.

"No trick at all, Bishop Walker. It seems you will be our guest for a while. Have you perchance a tin of Altoids?"

"Are you insane?" the bishop said, ignoring the last question. "You'll never get away with this. As soon as my pilot finishes his snack ..."

"Your pilot is also our guest, Bishop. He walked into a welcoming committee of ten armed men. I very much doubt he'll be visiting us any time soon."

"But ..." the high clergyman blustered. "You said you and Brother Coyle were close to reaching an arrangement."

"Oh, that we are, that we are indeed, *Preacher* Walker," Manuel said, lowering the bishop's station by several ranks. Only the negotiating parties haven't so much been the church and the buyer. You see, the buyer is Coast Conglomerates as represented by that pale little man sitting on the sofa. His name is Terry Prince. We've been, ah, discussing an arrangement where Coast Conglomerates turns the factory and the land over to us."

"*Us*, as in us, the church?"

"Us, as in your hosts, an advance guard of Hispanic-American settlers who intend to set up our own town in Libertyville."

"To do what?" the bishop sneered. "To cook rice and beans? To import cocaine? Isn't that what you people do best?"

Manuel answered him by a sharp slap across the face. Bishop Walker was stunned, not so much by the force of the blow, but by the audacity, the nerve of a lowly ... whatever he was ... peasant putting on airs. "How *dare* you!"

That comment was answered by another slap, a harder one, to the other cheek. "You want to try for more, Mister Walker, you lame horse's ass excuse for a clergyman?"

The bishop was not about to give up his high moral ground. "You think you can somehow drag me down to your level with your bullying tactics, you son of a whore? Lest you forget, I am one of Christ's representatives on earth, you … you *scum*."

Calm yourself, Manuel's inner conscience cautioned him. *You're losing it. If you let this pompous Negrón get to you, you'll lose face in front of the white man, the old gringo, the other Negrón, and your own people.* But the other part of his thought process was furious. *That bastardo is challenging me, my manhood. If I let him get away with this, I will be no better than a castrato in front of my people.*

The two men, each a self-appointed leader from a different world, which was actually the same world, the world of the dispossessed, glared balefully at one another. The tension rose with every second ticked off by the old Regulator clock in the far corner of the room. Manuel slowly withdrew the sidearm from its holster and raised it until it was aimed directly at the clergyman's head.

"Can you give me one reason, just one very good reason, why I should not end this confrontation very satisfactorily and very finally?" he addressed the bishop.

"As a matter of fact, I can give you several very good reasons."

Every head in the room snapped in the direction of the new voice, whose owner stood calmly at the door, a nasty-looking submachine gun in his hands.

"Brother Luke? Saints be praised. How on earth did you manage to escape those … those assassins in the commissary?"

"Very simple, Your Excellency. I never went to the commissary. Some second sense told me things might go better if you had a bit

CHAPTER 14

of help. When you gentlemen got into the elevator, I returned to the helicopter. We're always equipped for such contingencies, aren't we, Bishop Walker?"

"Indeed," the portly bishop said. "The good Lord doth provide."

"How...?" Manuel started to ask.

"Brother Luke is not only my pilot. He's been my eyes and ears and my personal bodyguard for the past dozen years. Before that, he was a marine sniper, the most dangerous animal in that jungle we call society, Mister Alcantar." The bishop glanced around the room. Neither Manuel, José, nor Hernán had lowered their weapons. Two rifles were pointed at Brother Luke. Manuel's pistol remained aimed at Bishop Walker's head. Luke's submachine gun was aimed in the direction of Manuel Cabrera. No one moved. A brittle silence hung heavily between them.

The Regulator clock continued its steady ticking, the loudest sound in the room.

The silence was punctuated by a frantic voice behind Luke. "*Lider, lider!*" It was a young Mexican who'd come running up the stairs from the cafeteria. "Please, you must come quickly. There is more fighting downst –"

In less than a second, Luke turned sharply to his right. Without a conscious thought, he drilled a burst of fire into the Mexican, pulping his head and killing him instantly. Concurrently, the lblast from Hernán's rifle ended Luke's life.

In the melee that followed, Terry Prince succeeded in grabbing the submachine gun, which remained cradled in his arms for two seconds before a hard kick to his groin from José knocked him to the floor, howling in the most brutal pain he'd experienced in his life. The bishop lunged for the weapon, but Manuel delivered a well-aimed fist to his midsection, causing a loud *whooshing* noise. Bishop Walker sagged onto the couch.

In the confusion of the moment, Moses Mendelssohn quietly walked over to the middle of the office and seized the master weapon. "Gentlemen," he intoned. The room suddenly became quiet once again. "It seems we are deadlocked. What better time can there be to sit down and talk like *civilized* men?"

Each of the combatants looked around the room at the two dead bodies. Hispanic, African-American, and white stared fixedly at one another, not knowing what would come next.

At that moment, Moses Mendelssohn dropped the submachine gun, grasped at his chest, and fell moaning to the ground, his breathing rapid and shallow.

15

Letitia Coyle was frantic. Four-thirty and no word from Augustus. She'd been trying to telephone the plant for the past two hours. The constant busy signal had nearly driven her crazy with worry. The factory was two miles from the church. Augustus had taken their only car. The rain had continued on and off during the afternoon. The road was a quagmire. The marshland to the side of the road was even worse. Unless one had access to a four- wheel-drive vehicle or a helicopter Libertyville was an island, isolated from the rest of the world.

൭൨

"Madison, Roy Kemp here. Weather seems to be gettin' worse. You ready to go over to the factory?"

"Be about ten, fifteen minutes. Didn't you say you walked over there earlier this mornin'?"

"Yeah, but that was *much* earlier. On'y way anybody can get anywhere now is if'n you got a four-wheel drive. Man, you are one smart sonofabitch, buyin' Glenn Riley's old Jeep Cherokee last year. I'll see you in fifteen."

Kemp had just replaced the phone on its cradle when it rang again.

"Mister Kemp, this is Letitia Coyle. I hate to disturb you on a terrible Saturday afternoon like this, but my husband has gone missing since ten-thirty this morning, and I haven't heard a word from him. The phone at the factory has been busy for hours and I'm worried sick. I have this horrible feeling something's wrong over at the cotton works. I know you live close by, –"

"Mrs. Coyle, there's no way to get over to the factory on foot, even if I wanted to. Madison Peebles is one of the few people in town with a four-wheeler, and he's coming to pick me up in about fifteen minutes. I'll get him to swing by your place on the way to the factory.

෴

"How much farther, Sarah?"

"Half an hour. I've got to take it much slower than usual. Anything over twenty-five and this car will fishtail all over the road, even if it's an ATV."

"And your premonition?"

"Stronger than ever, Mordechai. In my bones I feel something *has* happened. It wasn't that way until fifteen minutes ago. Who knows? Maybe God will reward you for coming up here with me."

෴

"Any of you a medico?" Manuel asked, the first to emerge from the shock of what had happened.

No one responded.

"Okay, let's all of us think for a moment. Mendelssohn's last words before he … before whatever happened to him, was that we should sit down and talk like civilized men. Each of us seems to have our own agenda here. We're fighting over the bones of Mendelssohn's company and unless we do something pretty damned quick, we're going to be fighting over the bones of *Mendelssohn*."

"May I make an observation, Mister Bragado?"

"Go ahead, Reverend Coyle."

"Mister Mendelssohn got possession of the biggest weapon. He could have taken control, yet he made no attempt to use it or threaten anyone. After he had his attack, none of us was in a great hurry to retrieve that weapon, so that means we're back to where we were ten minutes ago. You and your two friends have the guns, so you're back in control."

"That's so."

"It's pretty obvious we disagree about everything, primarily who gets this factory and the land around it. We've all got a vested interest here, except Moses Mendelssohn. He sold out to a buyer who's got a signed contract. I understand the contract provides that Mister Mendelssohn'll be taken care of financially for the rest of his life, but after that there's no further payment required. If Mister Mendelssohn dies now, the buyer's made a very good deal indeed."

"That was not the intent," Terry Prince said.

"No one said it was, Mister Prince," Reverend Coyle continued. "What I'm trying to say is that Moses Mendelssohn is the only one in this room who does not have a vested interest. He's an innocent victim of *our* war, but it's not *his* war, no matter what happens. In every war going back to Biblical times there were a few very special times when the combatants on both sides declared a temporary cease fire to enable the injured and the innocent to be cleared out, evacuated to a safe distance from the battleground. Human beings have never shown themselves to be particularly humane, but that's one example where, no matter what the time or place, man showed his best self."

"You're saying we should declare a temporary cease fire to get Mendelssohn to where he can receive medical help?"

"Exactly."

Manual Cabrera pondered the idea for a few moments. "And when he's gone?"

"We continue doing what we came here to do. Fight to the death if that's the only way we can resolve our dispute."

"That means we're going to have to trust one another, even if it's for a few minutes." He glared at the bishop, who, sat like a smug Buddha, an inscrutable half-smile on his face. "Obviously I don't trust *him*," Cabrera said. "It's a shame his pilot had to be killed instead of him. We could've used the chopper to ferry Mendelssohn to the nearest medical facility."

"Rather a unique time for you to be preaching morality, Mister Alcantar, although I doubt that's your real name," the bishop spoke up haughtily.

Manuel ignored the bishop, as if he were of no greater moment than a mouse turd on the floor. "Mister Prince?"

"It would have to be one of your men to take him anywhere. You must be aware there's no doctor in Libertyville."

"I am."

"That means the nearest place would be Tomkinsville. Ten miles up the road, ten miles of mud, silt, and crud. Figure at least an hour in the best of circumstances and it's going to be a rough ride no matter what vehicle's available."

"So it's agreed that one of our men should drive him?"

"I don't see any alternative," Augustus said.

For the first time, a shadow of doubt crossed Manuel Cabrera's face. He could trust himself and he could trust José, but other than that, he'd only known the rest of his vanguard for a very short time. They'd already proved untrustworthy, not once but twice, in the span of an hour. Most of them didn't even own a car, so it would be the easiest thing in the world to appropriate the car they were assigned, dump the old man in a ditch, and take off for parts unknown. Besides, as hungry and desperate as they were, he had no doubt they might well resort to killing one another in order to get the coveted job of leaving what was turning out to be a hellhole.

He looked around the room, weighing the alternatives. *The white guy would get Mendelssohn to wherever he needed to be, but his next stop would be the police, and who're the police going to believe as between a bunch of dirty Mexicans, the local preacher of a poor African-American church, a bishop who looked like the white man's perception of stereotype African "royalty," and a WASP company man?* That eliminated Prince.

The only one he trusted was the Black preacher man – not the pompous asshole bishop, but the younger guy, who seemed like a genuinely decent sort. But could he be trusted to return once he'd left? Manuel thought if he were in the same position as Reverend Coyle, he'd drop Mendelssohn off and keep straight on going, as far away as he could get from Libertyville.

At that moment, Manuel saw two vehicles, a white Audi All Terrain Vehicle and a nondescript Jeep Cherokee, pull into the parking lot almost simultaneously. "Any of you *hombres* recognize either of those SUVs?"

Bishop Walker, Reverend Coyle, and Terry Prince looked out the window. As they were looking, the inhabitants started to exit the vehicles. Prince shrugged his shoulders. "Nope."

Manuel said, "I recognize the fat white guy from this morning. Roy Kemp, the night watchman. There're two women, one white, one Black, a bearded guy, and an old Black man who doesn't look to be in much better shape than Mendelssohn."

As Augustus Coyle studied the vehicles, he started to tremble.

"Something wrong, Brother Coyle?" the bishop said, a look of smug superiority on his face.

"Please don't –"

"Don't what, Brother Coyle? Don't tell the assembly about the little problem this presents for you?" His smile was mirthless and evil.

"What're you talking about, Clergyman?" Manuel interrupted.

"Oh, nothing … nothing at all. You might want to ask Brother Coyle, who's obviously become your buddy."

Reverend Coyle looked helpless, hopeless.

"It's all right, *compadre*," Manuel said, trying to comfort the distraught Augustus. "You wanna' tell me about it? You don't have to if you don't want to."

"Thank you, Señor Bragado. I appreciate your sensitivity."

"Sensitivity? Did I hear you say 'sensitivity' Brother Coyle? I wonder how friendly your new buddy would be if he knew the real reason you're all trembly. Mister Alcantar, you may as well know the Black woman's his wife, the mother of his two little chilluns, and he's been pokin' the white woman for the past two years – getting' a little unauthorized pussy on the side."

"Shut up," Augustus said tightly.

"The truth will set you free, my son," the bishop continued. "Yessir, our young holier-than-thou Augustus Coyle may be about to get his comeuppance. Interesting that the two ladies in his life converge on us at this propitious mo – "

The bishop gasped as Coyle reared back and punched him hard on the jaw.

"Why you ungracious sonofabitch! You disgrace to the cloth! You immoral, fornicating plague on the church! As of this moment you are summarily –"

CHAPTER 15

"Excommunicated? Is that what you want to say, you fat fraud?" Augustus was breathing hard. "You think I give a rat's ass for you and your church? Is that the way you think a man of God should act? Jesus said, 'Let he who is without sin cast the first stone.' Well you listen right here, Mister William Wyatt Walker, you think I don't know you've been screwing your brains out whenever you get the chance? You think I haven't heard the rumors of you and the little choir boys? You think I don't see you preaching God's holiness and the dignity of poverty while you watch to make sure your girls in the back room count every last nickel of the five hundred million dollars the church steals from the poor each year?" He was gasping. Every eye on the room was now on the two Black men. Even Mendelssohn was watching the scene. The silence was palpable.

"Gentlemen," Moses said softly, in a wheezing voice. All eyes turned to the old man. "In a situation like this, your Jesus would have preached forgiveness. I've lived a long life, going from defeat to defeat to defeat, until in the end I realized that the ultimate victory lies not at some high point along the way, but in having made the journey. Bishop Walker, Reverend Coyle, trust me, no matter how serious this all seems now, in a few years – so very few years – it will be meaningless. You'll end up like me. Ten years after that no one except your relatives will even remember you walked the earth."

Manuel Cabrera looked long and hard at Mendelssohn. Then he looked at the rest of the men in the room. "Isn't it amazing that in a sea of discord it's the voice of calm that's the island?"

"I'm sorry, Your Excellency," said Augustus. "Forgive me."

The bishop stood still for a moment, looking around the room. Then he pronounced in a soft and terrible voice, "Mister Coyle, the church has rules. I am the interpreter of those rules, the court of last resort. I cannot, and I will not revoke the excommunication and the shredding of your vestments that entails. I will pray for your salvation in the next life."

The room went silent again. The silence was icy. It was Terry Prince who finally spoke. "Bishop Walker, you are an embarrassment to your church, an embarrassment to the brotherhood of man, and a disgrace the human race. You are quick to condemn because somewhere in that insecurity that's at the core of your being you must raise your own status on the shoulders of others who are, in every way, better men than you will ever hope to be. It is because of sanctimonious frauds like you, whose God is better than the other man's God, that there will never be peace on this earth."

"Gentlemen," Manuel said, "while we're standing around arguing about morals and morality, a good man could be dying. Those people outside are our best hope of getting Mister Mendelssohn the help that may keep him alive, but they won't remain outside for long. All we need is for them to come in here and survey this scene – the guns, the blood, the bodies – and then we'll have to hold them hostage or do away with them altogether. I'm sorry, but that reality's more urgent than our argument." He looked at his surviving lieutenant. "Yes, José?"

"*Lider*, it will take three men to lift Señor Mendelssohn and carry him to the elevator. We must take him to them. They will know what to do to help. It is the only decent thing to do."

"I agree, *compadre*," Manuel said quietly. "Which three?"

"You, me, and the *Negrón* – the Reverend, not the bishop."

"A good idea. That leaves Hernán, Mister Prince, and the other …" Such was his disdain for the bishop that he didn't even say his name. "Hernán, can you take care of the situation?"

The third Hispanic looked uncertain. "I don't know, *lider*, I have been twenty-four hours without food or sleep."

"It will only be ten, perhaps fifteen minutes, *amigo*," Manuel said gently. "You are a lion. You will be carrying the hopes and dreams of a whole town that is to be. I trust you, *muchacho*."

"Thank you, *lider*. I will not let you down."

CHAPTER 15

"Mister Mendelssohn, please help us if you can," Manuel said, standing close to the old man so he could be clearly heard. "Is there anything – a cot, a flat board? – anything we could use to transport you down to the cars?"

"Yes," Mendelssohn said calmly. "Down the hall, in Madison Peebles' office, there's a storage room. There's a small cot against the far wall."

Within two minutes, José had returned with a lightweight folding cot. He, Manuel, and Augustus lifted Moses Mendelssohn and placed him on the cot. Mendelssohn was starting to fade into unconsciousness. His skin had turned clammy and he was shivering. "Are you going to be sick, Mister Mendelssohn?" Manuel asked.

"No, no." Mendelssohn wheezed. "You think I'll make it to heaven, Reverend Gus?" he asked, turning toward the town's clergyman.

"If I was God, there'd be no question you would," Augustus replied. "But you know what, Mister Mendelssohn? I wouldn't recite the *kaddish* for you yet," he said, referring to the Jewish prayer over the dead. "As long as you're breathin', there's hope. Sarah's here."

"Sarah?" The old man came awake with a start and smiled. "I've never thought of her as the angel of death."

"Is she his only relative?" Manuel asked.

"Only one anyone knows about," Augustus replied.

"Reverend Gus," Mendelssohn said, "can you lean closer so you can hear me?"

"Of course, Mister Mendelssohn." He bent toward the old man's head.

"Reverend Gus, I heard everything everybody's been saying. Is it true? Have you and Sarah been …?"

"Yes, Mister Mendelssohn."

"Well, son, I've never been one to sit in judgment on another human being. God knows if somebody judged me, I'd sure be found wanting. All I want to say is, I don't know what led you to her, but if you've brought her some happiness, that makes me happy. Regardless of how or what, if for just a moment in your lives … I'm proud she hooked up with someone like you. If it was a momentary lapse, you're only a human being and you're entitled to it."

The bishop, who had been listening, breathed in deeply and pulled himself to his full height. "I heard what you said, Old Man," he said, his voice raised so that Mendelssohn could not miss a word. "You're proud that Brother … that Mister Coyle has, as you put it, 'hooked up' with your niece? *You* are proud that one of your own, a *Jewish* harlot, spawn of a race of Christ killers hooked up with one of *ours*? I believe *your* people think they're the chosen people and that African-Americans – what your race so arrogantly chooses to call *schvartzes* – Niggers – are so far down the totem pole that your people are doing us a favor by lowering yourselves to even *talk* to us."

"I never felt that way about any other human being," Moses said. "There are good people and bad people in every race and culture. You may not believe this, Bishop Walker, but there were good people in Germany during the Nazi days. Germans who risked their lives to feed a Jew or a Gypsy, to give them a crust of bread or a plate of soup, even to hide them."

"Ah, aren't you the expert on human beings?" the bishop said. "Let me tell you right now, Mister Mendelssohn, I have never been a hypocrite and I've always spoken the truth as I see it. So I will say it again. Your niece, your Jewish harlot, has been lying with a married man, a man with two children, a man of God. She led him into temptation and you *dare* say she's delivered him from evil? Picture it, Old Man, or has it been so long since you've been able to get that shriveled thing of yours up? Picture them naked and wet and smelly and thrashing. A Black

CHAPTER 15

man and a white woman, like a grotesque chess game where the white pieces mingle with the black pieces until the whole game falls apart. Makes you sick to call it 'making love?' Try 'fornicating.' Try *'fucking.'* Like two animals in heat rutting. You see salvation in *that*, do you, you old hypocrite?"

Moses managed, with more difficulty than he had ever felt in his life, to bring himself to a sitting position. "I shall give you a benediction, Bishop," he said, wheezing. "Can you come a bit closer?"

"*You* want to give *me* a benediction? Who are *you* to presume to have the gall to give me a blessing?" The bishop looked around. Every eye in the room was glaring at him. "Oh, very well," he said. "Tell me what you have to say?"

"Just this." The old man, with an almost superhuman effort, breathed in as deeply as could, hawked up a wad of saliva in his mouth, and spat full in the bishop's face.

The bishop instinctively flung back his arm and slapped the old man's face hard. As Moses Mendelssohn, sagged into semi-consciousness, Manuel lifted his rifle and aimed it directly at the bishop. He was just about to discharge the weapon when a quiet but authoritative voice commanded, "Please put the gun down, sir. More violence won't solve anything at this moment."

16

"Who are you? How did you get here, and just who do you think you are giving me orders?" Manuel asked, more surprised than outraged.

The tall, bearded man raised both hands, palms outward, and smiled gently. "The answer to your first question depends on whom you ask, sir. Some call me 'Rabbi,' although I'm not formally ordained. I started out life as Mark Davis, but nowadays I'm called Mordechai ben Zvi."

Manuel put down his rifle, but remained ready to pick it up in an instant.

The bishop rose from the armchair and approached ben Zvi. "Ah, a man of God, I trust? Someone to whom I can relate. Someone who understands the base instincts that cause a man and woman to lower themselves to the gutter, to profane themselves and the earth they inhabit."

"Aren't you being a little hard on mankind, sir? I'm afraid I didn't catch your name."

"William Wyatt Walker, Bishop of the Worldwide Church of Christ."

"I see," Mordechai said mildly. "Does that title somehow make you better than your parishioners and those you perceive as sinners?"

"Absolutely, Rabbi. Wouldn't you agree?"

"No."

CHAPTER 16

The Regulator clock continued to ignore the tension in the room and ticked on imperturbably. The last vestiges of daylight were fading as the long November night approached.

Mordechai turned and faced Manuel. "I've been outside the door listening for the past few minutes. To answer your second question, Mister Mendelssohn's niece Sarah had a premonition something was wrong with her uncle. That premonition got stronger as the afternoon progressed, so I agreed to drive up from the university with her. When we pulled into the parking lot, Mister Peebles, Mister Kemp, and Mrs. Coyle were in a vehicle just in front of us."

"How did you manage to get in here?" José asked.

"The others decided I was the most expendable person if there was any trouble. They thought since I was a man of the cloth, I'd be the least likely to be attacked. Long ago I suffered such a tremendous loss that if something were to happen to me, it would certainly be less than what happened back then, so I simply walked in the front door and up the stairs. When I got to the second floor, I heard loud voices above me. I figured if anything was happening it probably was happening up here. So, here I am."

"No one tried to stop you?" This from Manuel.

"No. Of course, I was walking rather quietly." He pointed to his rubber-soled tennis shoes. "And I imagine any noise I made was more than covered up by what's going on here. Are there more people in the building?"

"A few, Señor, but they're not your concern," Manuel said, his tone flat, but not unfriendly.

"Might I ask your name, Sir?"

"Of course, I am Maximilian Bragado-Galba y Alcantar."

"A Madrileño?"

Manuel looked surprised. "How would you know that?"

"May we speak in confidence, Señor Bragado?"

"I see no reason why not? Where do you suggest?"

"Just outside the hearing of the rest."

Manuel had not left the room for several hours. He was as hungry and tired as his troops, but he dared not show weakness in front of them. "José, Hernán," he addressed his compatriots. "Keep an eye on our guests. Señor ben Zvi and I wish to talk in private for a few moments."

✣

The six men remaining in the room sat or stood in uncomfortable silence. The bishop asked his hosts, "Have any provisions been made if one needs to use the necessaries?"

"Huh? Oh, you mean the toilet. I suppose there's no harm in you using it. Keep the door ajar, however. We don't want you escaping." Hernán laughed raucously as he tried to picture the large, clumsy man attempting to make his grand exit through a tiny third floor window.

As soon as the bishop was ensconced in the bathroom, he turned on the taps in the sink. When the water was running, he reached inside his robes and extracted a small, portable CB radio. Hoping its range would reach the nearest branch of the church in Tomkinsville, he radioed, "Breaker. Walker. Trouble. Libertyville. Need reinforcements immediately." The bishop stored the cumbersome unit back inside his robe, completed his toilet, and returned to the room.

✣

"All right *Jehudi*," Manuel said. "You wanted to talk. Proceed."

"Very well. So you changed your name, too?"

CHAPTER 16

"I would be careful what you say, Señor. I am armed."

Mordechai switched to fluent Spanish, but of an entirely different dialect than that spoken by Manuel. "And lest you forget, Señor Bragado," he said, in a quiet voice that did not carry more than two or three feet, "I really don't care. If you shoot me, you simply end my physical life ten years after I died anyhow. You know I mean you no harm. I don't know what's going on in there and I can assure you it's none of my business."

For the first time that day, Manuel was unnerved. He laid his rifle on the ground and stepped away from it. "You're right. This is not your concern. Does this show you I recognize you're not a part of this?"

"It makes me feel I may be able to leave your war zone with most of my parts intact." He laughed. "What part of Oaxaca province are you from?"

"How …?"

"Not difficult," Mordechai said, switching to colloquial Mexican Spanish. "I took Spanish in high school. After I graduated university, but before I met … someone … I spent a year backpacking through Mexico. My Castilian Spanish, of which I was so proud, wasn't worth a damn in the small villages and mountain towns. So I learned the language the people spoke, rather than the language I'd learned in school. It wasn't long before I could distinguish the difference between the Merida dialect and that spoken in Yucatan."

"You are a very clever man."

"What I did was nothing that could not be done by anyone. Your English, for example, is outstanding. Someone who had not studied people and their language very carefully would easily mistake you for a native of Madrid. May I ask candidly – and I give you my word it will go no farther than this hallway – what is going on in there?"

Manuel thought for a long moment before he answered. It was clear this man was completely unafraid of him, but was he trustworthy? If Manuel and his group were successful and established a beachhead in Libertyville, they would eventually have to interact with the local populace. He stared into Mordechai's eyes. All he could see was openness and acceptance. "Señor ben Zvi," he said slowly, "you are indeed observant."

"That's me, an 'observant Jew,'" Mordechai said. Manuel caught the double meaning immediately. The comment was so inane that it completely broke the tension and he enjoyed the first natural laugh he'd had all day. Such was the break in the stress level, the catharsis, that Manuel had to catch his breath and breathe deeply several times to get his bearing. He knew that when the intensity of the moment created so much tension, sometimes the most meaningless comment, even one that was not particularly funny or amusing, could be the pin that pricked the balloon of emotion and unleashed completely uncontrollable gales of laughter. The kind that, if you tried to make the same statement under different circumstances, wouldn't be remotely funny.

"Manuel Cabrera," he said, extending his hand.

"I'm sorry. Did you say Maximilian Bragado-Galba y Alcantar?"

That set Manuel to laughing once again, but neither so long nor so hard.

"A territorial fight?"

"You might say that. Mister Mendelssohn sold the plant to a large company in Atlanta. That company's represented by the short Anglo. The Worldwide Church of Christ wants the same plot of land for its headquarters. First it was the Reverend, the younger man, but now the older guy has taken over. My people – there are thirteen of us in the building – want the property so we can establish a place of our own. We have the guns and the ammunition – for now."

"But you see things spinning of control?"

"I could never say that to my *muchachos*. They claim they'd follow me to the end of the earth, but there's already been trouble. We'd planned to stay here and complete our takeover within the week. We were supposed to have plenty of food to last us that long. By that time, a hundred reinforcements would arrive, then another hundred, and by then we'd have a foothold in Libertyville. But the food van never showed up. The men haven't eaten for nearly twenty-four hours. They're tired. They're frustrated…"

"And you fear they could mutiny?"

"Some of them already have."

The two men stood in companionable silence for a few moments. Mordechai spoke first. "Do you feel there's a solution?"

"Not really. There should be, though. I'm a lawyer by training and by trade, and we're taught there's always a solution. If you mean cut up forty acres into thirds, that works very well in theory, but it doesn't take into consideration the prejudices that make this situation almost impossible to resolve. Even if we struck a deal, how long do you think it would last? Do you really believe Palestinians and Israelis will ever find common ground?"

"Everyone hopes."

"You really believe that? Think of the vested interests that want the instability to continue. You know why Hitler was able to whip the Germans up into such a frenzy against the Jews?"

"I see your point, Señor Bragado. I can only wish you good luck. As I said, it's not my battle. If you think I'll broadcast this to the authorities, or even to the people I'm with, I can promise you that won't happen."

"I believe you, Mister Ben Zvi."

"It's not a matter of trust or belief, Señor Bragado. It's a matter of survival. The less they know, the better."

"Agreed." Manuel reached out and shook hands warmly with ben Zvi. "We'd better return to the office. The old man needs help very badly. Any moment could be his last."

17

"Gentlemen," Manuel addressed the group. "Mister Mendelssohn's had some kind of attack. Someone's got to get him medical help, and quickly."

"It is the Lord's decree that he must face Judgment Day."

"Shut up, Mister Walker, or you may very shortly be facing Judgment Day," José said.

"I heard him talking about Sarah Coben and the Reverend Coyle," Mordechai said. "Called her a Jewish harlot and a whore. Reverend Coyle heard it too."

"Why not ask him?" the bishop said, undeterred.

"Very well, if it satisfies your voyeuristic instincts, Bishop. Reverend?"

Augustus, who had been stretched as taut as a man can be, started weeping. "Forgive me, Father ... Rabbi..." he blubbered.

"So it's true?"

"Y...yes."

"All right, you're forgiven. Now let's move on to more important things."

"What?" roared the bishop. "Who are *you* to absolve this sinner?"

"Who are *you* to *condemn* him?" Mordechai roared back, mimicking the bishop's tone. "Reverend Coyle is no more a sinner than you,

Bishop Walker. I challenge you, swear by your almighty God, swear by Christ, bishop that you have never strayed from your marriage bed."

"You, you heathen! You apostate! I don't intend to answer your blasphemous question! You *dare* accuse *me*? Someone whose position is sufficient to confirm his character? You … you Jewish piece of shit! Hitler should have finished the job so you need not have been born."

The springs of tension in the room had been wound tighter. Manuel was close to breaking. Hernán gripped the barrel of his gun and started to swing it like a baseball bat. Moses Mendelssohn moaned softly, not comatose, but close. All eyes in the room focused on Mordechai ben Zvi, who incongruously seemed relaxed, a slow smile spreading on his face. "Well, bishop, it appears you've given us an honest answer in front of seven witnesses. I think we've all got more important things on our minds now. Señor Bragado, how do you propose we deal with Mister Mendelssohn?"

"Before you came, I was debating who we could send down to carry Mister Mendelssohn to one of the vehicles. I trust Hernán and José, of course. The only other one I could think of was Reverend Coyle, but I wondered whether once he was out the door he'd be gone, and what would we do then? Now that you're here …"

"The most important thing is that we get Mister Mendelssohn to someone who might – *might* – save his life if we're in time. He's not part of your war. Reverend Coyle may have been a soldier in his church, but it seems he's been relieved of active duty by his superior, so he's no longer part of the war. In fact, if I were to guess, I'd say that Reverend Coyle would like to spend some healing time with his wife. I wouldn't be the least bit surprised if this was his last night in Libertyville and the coming of the new day will witness the *going* of Augustus Coyle. Am I right, Mister Coyle?"

"You got that right," Augustus said, the tension draining out of him like air from a tired balloon.

"You betrayer, you lowly scum," the bishop intoned. "You abandon your church in its time of need, you abandon your fellow man, and you abandon Christ."

Augustus turned and faced the bishop. For the first time that afternoon, the younger man was smiling. "I guess you can say that's true," he said. "I am not abandoning *my* church, I'm abandoning *your* church. Yes, Bishop Walker, I feel pretty darned good."

He turned on his heel and picked up one corner of the cot on which Moses Mendelssohn lay. "Gentlemen, may I respectfully ask for your help?" he said.

He was immediately joined by José, Hernán, and Mordechai. The four of them, bearing Moses Mendelssohn, left the room. Bishop Walker, frustrated and furious, stormed after them. Manuel stood with his rifle across his chest, barring the bishop's path.

"Get away from me, you heathen brown man," he said, shoving the astonished Manuel to the side. "Don't you dare try to stop me from doing justice and telling that poor good woman exactly what her husband has been doing behind her back."

Suddenly there was a sound that was unfathomable, something between a buzz and a growl, and Manuel, who was in process of lifting his rifle, stopped to stare. Little Terry Prince was running at the much larger bishop. With a whoop, the small man jumped on the bishop's back, clawing at his eyes and his throat. The enraged bishop thinking he would easily shake the man from Coast Conglomerates off his back like an elephant would have gotten rid of a pesky gnat, twisted around and moved toward the nearest wall, prepared to mash Prince against it. He might have done so, had not Manuel smacked him in the face with the rifle butt. Walker sank to the ground, unconscious.

ஐ

"Augustus!" Sarah and Letitia cried, almost simultaneously as the four men emerged from the building, bearing Moses Mendelssohn on the makeshift palanquin. Letitia looked at the other woman, wondering how Sarah would know her husband.

"Mrs. Coyle, your husband and I have shared a mutual respect for one another since he started guest lecturing at Barrymore State University," Sarah said smoothly. "I teach in the history department there, and African-American Emergence is the farthest thing in the college from my course in medieval and romance history."

Mordechai ben Zvi was equally swift on the uptake. Grabbing Sarah's arm in his best proprietorial manner, he said, "Sarah even convinced me to attend one of Reverend Gus' lectures three months ago."

"I never knew my husband was so famous," Letitia said. "Seems you have a following outside of Libertyville, Augustus."

Augustus looked at the ground modestly. Sarah thought, *how attractive his wife is.*

"What's happenin' in there?" Madison interjected.

"Negotiations are going hot and heavy over the cotton works and the forty acres," Augustus said.

"Moses told me he done already sold the business."

"That he did," Mordechai said, "but there's been interest from other sources, and those other sources have been sitting up in Mister Mendelssohn's office negotiating what we might call a 'secondary market' all day."

"Is everything all right?" Kemp asked nervously.

"Was," Augustus said. "Since Mister Mendelssohn collapsed, we've been trying to figure how we were going to get him medical assistance."

"Closest place is Tomkinsville," Madison said, "ten miles up the road. County Regional Clinic and Infirmary's four miles the other side of town. 'Course in this weather, that's serious travelin'."

CHAPTER 17

"We've got to get him there, sooner rather than later," Sarah said, assuming command of the situation. "Whose whirlybird is that?"

"Belongs to the church," Augustus said. "The bishop came down earlier this afternoon to join in the negotiations." *And tried to destroy me.*

"That provides an easy answer to our problem, Reverend Coyle," she said. "Did he fly it himself?"

"No. His pilot flew him down from Birmingham."

"In this weather, that helicopter is a gift from God," she said. "We needn't spend an hour or more slogging through these roads to get to some community clinic. We could fly him down to University of South Alabama Medical Center Hospital in Montgomery within the hour. Where's the pilot?"

José Sandoval shrugged. "He told us one of the rotors froze just after he put down in the parking lot, and asked if he could use one of our cars. Mister Bragado, the head of our negotiating team, loaned him the keys to the Toyota Land Cruiser. Since I don't see it in the lot, he's probably gone wherever he needed to go to get the part."

"So option number one is out," Mordechai said. "Back to the drawing board."

"Looks like we're stuck with Tomkinsville," Sarah said. "The Audi and the Jeep Cherokee are both four-wheel drive vehicles. If Mordechai and I drive up, there's no reason for you to follow us."

"Miz Sarah, Moses and me, we been friends for more almost half a century. If he's gonna' be okay, I wanna' be with him, and if he's gonna' pass ... well ..." old Madison broke down and started weeping. Pulling himself together, he continued, "If he's gonna' pass, I figger I should be there, too."

"I understand, Madison," she said walking over and putting her arms around his thin, quaking shoulders. "There's no need for all of us to go up to Tomkinsville."

"I'd like to go but I really can't," Letitia said. "The girls are at my mother's and they'll go wild if I'm not there to put them to bed at night."

"It's getting darker by the minute," Augustus said.

"Reverend Coyle, your place is with your wife," Sarah said firmly. "So why don't we do this? Mister Peebles, you drive Reverend and Mrs. Coyle and Mister Kemp home. It won't take more than a few minutes to do that. You know the way to the Clinic and we don't, so we'll follow you to Tomkinsville."

"That's a good idea, Miz Sarah. I'm sure you'll be able to keep up with me, 'cause I won't be goin' very fast in this weather."

"Then it's done. Should we put my uncle in the back seat of the Audi or the back of the Jeep?"

"Jeep'd be larger and flatter, so's he could stretch out."

"The Audi's not that much smaller and the back seat's more comfortable. I rode in the back of a Cherokee once. Ugh!"

"Have it your way," Peebles shrugged. "But I think we should be on our way."

"That's what we'll do then. It'll take me a couple of minutes to clear out the back," Sarah said. "I figured we'd spend the weekend with my uncle. From what I remember, he's not very generous with himself when it comes to food, so I brought enough food to feed an army for the weekend: three large salamis, five loaves of rye bread, a Costco-sized bag of salad greens, a gallon of potato salad, and a thermos full of coffee. I figured Uncle Moses would have a freezer full of food for a month."

Hearing about the food, José looked at Hernán, then back at Sarah. "Ms. Coben, if you're overloaded with food, there are people in Mister Mendelssohn's office who've been going at it a long time – all day, in fact. I was just wondering …?"

CHAPTER 17

"No problem, at all," Sarah replied. "Uncle Moses won't be needing that food *this* weekend. We'll probably be spending most of our time in Tomkinsville, or on the way down to Mobile or Montgomery. Help me get it out of the back, help me get my uncle into the back, and it's yours."

ഇോര

When José and Hernán returned to the office with their booty, they came upon a very flustered Manuel. "What's the matter, *lider?*" José asked.

"This," Manuel said, holding up the CB unit. "I found it when we searched him, after he conveniently fell asleep. I'm sure he's sent a message out. I don't know how he could have sent it. He's been under guard since he arrived."

Hernán looked down at the floor. "While you were down the hall, talking with the other man, the bishop had to go to the bathroom. I figured since you'd let everyone else go, as long as they kept the door ajar there was no harm. Come to think of it, he did stay in there rather a long time."

"Damn!" Manuel swore. "It would take only a few moments to send a message. He probably sent an alarm seeking reinforcements."

"I suppose I should say, 'Bravo,' Mr. Bragado," Prince said, "but somehow I don't feel much like celebrating. Maybe we could've worked something out, maybe not, but you could easily have killed everyone in the room by now and you didn't. I can't say I'd trust the bishop to be so decent."

"Well, *Amigos*," José said. "At least we've got some reinforcements, too."

"What do you mean?"

In response, José kicked his toe gently at the box he'd brought in. Manuel's eyes widened as he gazed in rapture at the feast. "There's enough for everyone," he said. "Even you, Mister Prince. *El Puerco* can afford to miss a meal, but how do we secure him?"

"Easy," José said. "Hernán and I will stay here. "Mister Prince, you can stay with us. We'll split a loaf of bread and enough of the salami to make a couple of sandwiches each. You take the rest down to our *compadres* in the cafeteria. I'm sure everyone will feel a lot better after this unexpected fiesta."

18

The church had used every connection it had to purchase five of the 2,334 High Mobility Multipurpose Wheeled Vehicles, which AM General had scheduled for delivery to the United States Army in 1985. As of 1989, hardly any civilian in America had set eyes on a "Hummvee." At just about the time Madison Peebles' Jeep was halfway between Libertyville and Tomkinsvlle, one of those five monsters was thundering down the County Road two miles northwest of Tomkinsville, oblivious to the heavy rain and the muddy surface. It was very big, very heavy, and very much the ruler of the road, and God help anyone who got in its way, particularly since, in a way, it was God's vehicle.

Inside the Hummvee were seven toughs, ranging from nineteen to twenty-three. When Bishop Walker's message had been relayed from Tomkinsville to the closest church center that possessed on of the behemoths, that office had responded immediately. Two of the land-monster's inhabitants, brothers as well as "Brothers," had grown up in Detroit's inner city. Three others had relocated north when Hurricane Katrina ripped through New Orleans. The other two were locals. The Hummvee was loaded with semi-automatic weapons, incendiary devices, and handguns. It was a rolling arsenal whose passengers had been lubricated during the drive by several bottles of Southern Comfort, bourbon, and brandy.

Rudolph Washington, the oldest of the bunch, was driving the Hummvee. Occasionally, he reached over to Jerome Berry, and swigged back a slug of the bourbon.

"Fuckin' assholes're goin' to find out what it's like to mess with the church," he said, chuckling nastily. "Where the motherfuck is this Libertyville anyway?"

"Ten miles south of Tomkinsville on some little shit side road," Jerome answered. "We gotta' game plan, Rudolph?"

"Nawww. All I was told was that Bishop Walker messaged for help. I s'pose him bein' a bishop and all, he'll tell us what we're gonna' do. Should be fun, though."

"Be nice if there were women down there," a voice came from the back of the SUV. "Man, this is the kinda' night that could be special. Beatin' up the bad guys and pussy as a ree-ward." There was loud laughter in the vehicle.

༺༻

"He cursed me out in front of that whole group and excommunicated me. I never felt so humiliated in my life."

"I'm so sorry it had to happen to you, darling," she said, rubbing against his arm. "We're on our way out of here tomorrow morning."

"I am so, so lucky to have you, kitten. What do you think of the bishop's idea?"

"It's monstrous, like some kind of perverted Disneyland. If they build this 'God's Country,' they'll soak even more money from the poor Blacks, while they get richer. You can bet they aren't going to have fifty-dollar-a-night rooms. I wouldn't put it past the church to try to put a casino in. 'Holy Rollers.'"

The two of them laughed. "On the plus side, they could bring this town back to life and provide employment. But on balance, what they propose is the worst possible thing they could do for the greatest number of sufferers."

"Amen, my beloved," she said. She looked at her watch. "Six o'clock. I was able to get mama on the phone. I told her I'd found you and we'd be back about seven, maybe seven-thirty."

"But we're already home. We could be over there in ten minutes …"

"We could," she said, rubbing harder against him. "Or we could find something else to do until seven-thirty."

"Such as?"

"Children play little people's games. I thought we could play big people's games."

"Fallen woman!"

"Not unless you push me. So we're really going to start a new life tomorrow?"

"Bet your bottom dollar."

She led him to the bedroom, where she slowly, seductively disrobed. "We'll have a lot to do tomorrow," she said huskily. "It's getting awfully hard to wait, lover. What say we start our private celebration right now?"

ဏည

"How far from Tomkinsville?"

"The odometer says four miles, Mordechai."

"How fast are we going?"

"Nine miles an hour. Even at that speed, the car feels as if it's dancing on toe shoes."

"How far ahead is Madison Peebles?"

"Can't even see him. I seem to recall there's some curves up ahead. I've got to slow down, Mordechai. We'll meet Madison when we got to Tomkinsville. I told him to meet us at the first traffic light."

Just then, a sudden strong gust of wind and rain struck the Audi, pushing it off the right side of the narrow road. The car leaned hard to its right, bogged down on the muddy shoulder and refused to budge.

"Damn!" Sarah swore. "Now we've really got trouble." She looked at the fuel gauge. "Almost empty. I wasn't planning on coming this far. The Shell station back in Libertyville was already closed." She turned the ignition off. "Now's not the time to panic. Let's think this through."

ഹോൾ

Madison Peebles' Jeep was a mile ahead of the Audi. He couldn't even see the Audi's headlights in rearview mirror. The square back of the Cherokee was so muddy he probably wouldn't have seen the car if it had been a quarter of a mile back. No problem. He'd meet them in Tomkinsville. The display clock read six thirty-five. He tried to concentrate on the road ahead. The windshield wipers were as old and tired as the Jeep. They hadn't been changed in three years. He could barely see twenty feet ahead of him, but it didn't matter. He'd driven this road so often in the last forty years he knew every curve and hill by heart.

ഹോൾ

"My *bravos,* I asked you to have faith. You did, and God has provided." As he looked around, Manuel saw that every one of his remaining *soldados* was sated and there was still enough food left over to get all of them through the noonday meal tomorrow. "My *toros,* we may soon be facing a new problem. The old fat *Negrón* may have called in his own *bastardos* to attack us. I don't know when they'll arrive. Many of you have gone without sleep for more than twenty-four hours, but no man can go on forever without rest. Find a comfortable spot, anyplace in this building. There are cots and sofas all over the place. You must sleep now. God will wake you up when it is time."

※

The bishop had been awake for half an hour. He sat complacently, a beatific smile on his face, saying nothing. He was immune from the glares of the two men guarding him. The boilers were still on, and the room was comfortably warm. "I fear I need to go to the restroom again."

"You can piss in your pants," Hernán said bitterly.

"At the very least you could offer me some sustenance. I believe it is the dinner hour and I couldn't help but notice that the two of you and my co-prisoner have eaten."

"You can starve."

"Lovely, lovely," the bishop commented wryly. "Very well, I'll simply wait on the food." He stood up, walked over to the corner of the room, lifted his robe, and loudly urinated on the wooden floor."

"You are truly disgusting," José said sourly.

"*I?* It was certainly not my doing that your associate chose to administer cruel and unusual punishment. When – if – you get to be my age, you will find that a man's needs when it comes to voiding oneself, are rather urgent. I could well have wet my pants, as your friend suggested, but then I would be uncomfortable and it would look unseemly. Besides, it would only be twenty minutes before I would have to go again."

"If it were up to me, I'd have killed you long ago," José said.

"How courageous. The voice of the coward who is elevated to bully when he has a weapon." He sighed. "I suppose that is the way of the world." He looked toward the Regulator clock. "Six forty-one. It shouldn't be too much longer."

"What do you mean, *Negrón*?"

"I believe we will shortly have company." José and Hernán looked around the room nervously. "Oh, you'll know when they arrive."

"How many?"

"Enough to more than even the odds. Mister Prince," he said, turning toward the Caucasian. "Now that that sniveling Augustus Coyle has chosen to leave us, it will soon be you and me. After these … pirates are dispensed with, it will be the appropriate time for us to continue these, er, negotiations."

ಸಬ

"Man, I thought we'd never get out of that chickenshit town," Rudolph said. "Now for some real fun. Dark night, muddy little road, hills, curves – roller coaster time. Any of you have any objection to me crankin' this baby up?" No one responded. "I'm gonna' gun it up to fifty. We should be where we need to be in twenty minutes."

"What if we leave the road, Brother?"

"You gettin' cold feet, Jerome?"

"No. Just askin'."

"This is a Hummvee, in case you haven't noticed. The big fuckin' war machine, the ultimate off-road motherfucker. It eats trees and rocks and shit like that for dinner."

"You're the driver, Rudolph."

CHAPTER 18

Rudolph Washington downshifted and made sure the four wheel drive was engaged. Then he accelerated. The fully-loaded Hummvee, its engine screaming, its huge all-terrain tires grabbing for purchase, bounced up and down and from side to side. Every thirty feet or so, it would swerve and leave the road. Then, the exuberant Rudolph Washington would correct and the beast tromped down the muddy road again. "Yeeeee-haaaaaa!" he shouted. "Fifty fuckin' miles an hour! We did it, baby! We gonna' carve us some ass when we get to Libertyville!"

ℰℜ

Less than a mile away, coming in the opposite direction, his windows closed, the heater blowing, Madison Peebles glanced at the clock on the instrument panel. Six forty-four. He needed companionship, any companionship. He turned on the radio and caught an oldies station out of Montgomery.

ℰℜ

"That was so-o-o- wonderful," Letitia sighed, her voice still husky, but now sleepy with fulfillment. "It hasn't been this good in … I can't remember when. I must've come a hundred times."

"Three," he said, softly stroking her nipples. "One for each child?"

"One for *each* child?"

"Darling, I'm sure we connected that time. Number three may just have started out five minutes ago."

"And if not?" she teased.

"Well, if at first you don't succeed …" They laughed, the tender, fulsome, soft laughter of two happily exhausted animals who, for an infinitesimal eternity, had become one.

"Six forty-five," Augustus said lazily, looking across his woman at the clock radio. "I'll go pick up the kids in a little while, but I want to lie here like this just a little longer. There's just enough light for me to see how absolutely gorgeous you are."

"Help!" she squealed. "The man's gone insane!" She reached down and pinched him playfully. "Bet you can't do it again."

"Now?"

"Right now!"

"Siren!"

"Ooooh-eee-ooooh-eee," she said, her voice rising and falling in imitation of a police vehicle.

"Okay, woman," he said, rolling over on top of her. "I'll show you your man can rise to the occasion."

ಐಡ

The Hummer rounded the corner at fifty. "Hey, Bro, don't you think you should slow d – ?" Jerome never finished the question.

Madison saw the lights of the larger vehicle exactly two seconds before the collision. But he never had the chance to count those seconds. And mercifully, he never lived to know what had hit him.

Neither did the seven men in the Hummvee. As it struck the Cherokee without slowing down, the huge military vehicle exploded with a thunderous boom, sending a shaft of incendiary fire thirty feet into the air, lighting up the dark sky like a giant meteor crashing to the earth.

There were no survivors. There was no way there could have been.

19

Sarah and Mordechai saw the flash, but the explosion was muted by the storm and the surrounding woods.

"What was that?" she asked, shuddering.

"Hard to tell," Mordechai replied. "I haven't seen any cars on this road. I'd say a power line probably came down, which is probably the best thing that could have happened."

"Why do you say that?"

"They'll close down the road between Libertyville and Tomkinsville. The state patrol will cruise the road from one end to the other to clear it of traffic, and that means they'll see us. Are you warm enough, Mister Mendelssohn?" he said, turning toward the back seat.

"No," he said. "Something terrible just happened. I can feel it." He trembled.

"I could turn on the motor and put the heater on full," Sarah said.

"Not a good idea if we're low on gas. In all that stuff you brought for our picnic, did you, perhaps, think to bring a blanket?"

"As a matter of fact, I did, Your Rabbi-ship," she said. "It's in the trunk."

"And I suppose you want me to fetch it?"

"You certainly don't expect a lady to walk around in this kind of rain, wind, and muck, do you?"

When Mordechai returned, windblown, wet, and cold, he managed to reach back and cover the old man. "Are you in pain, Mister Mendelssohn?"

"Not really," he said, his voice reedy. "Uncomfortable, but still among the living. Do either of you children have an aspirin and a glass of water?"

Mordechai looked at Sarah, who nodded. For the second time in as many minutes, he exited the front door on the passenger side, and slogged through deep mud to the trunk. He returned with two clear plastic bottles of spring water and a small bottle of aspirin. Mordechai handed Mendelssohn two aspirin and an open bottle of water. The old man drank thankfully and lay back, breathing fitfully.

"Something happened up ahead," Mendelssohn said. "Wasn't Madison ahead of us?"

"Yes, Uncle Moses. He's going to meet us in Tomkinsville."

"No, he won't," the old man said quietly, tears forming in his eyes.

"How do you know?" Mordechai asked.

"I know."

෨෬

Pearl Snedecker lived at the south end of Tomkinsville. Sixty-eight and a widow, she'd lived in the house for the last thirty-years. She and Henry had raised four kids, good kids, and they still came around at least once a week. She'd just opened a can of cat food and was about to put it down when Tucker, her tabby, yowled and jumped up on the kitchen counter. A moment later, she saw a bright flash to the south and heard a muted WHOOMPF.

"Gol' durn it, Tucker, we're about to lose electricity again. Some durn tree probably fell on a power line. We're lucky we don't have one

CHAPTER 19

of them newfangled electric phones. We got the old fashioned kind with the phone line that doesn't depend on no power line."

Two minutes passed. Pearl was surprised that the lights stayed on. "May as well call the cops anyway and alert 'em there's a tree down. They probably know it already, but it never hurts to be a good citizen, right, kitty?" Tucker brushed his head against her legs and purred as he walked by.

ಸಿಲ

By eight o'clock, Bishop Walker, was distinctly nervous. It was nearly four hours after he had signaled his headquarters to send reinforcements to this stinking rathole – *much* more than enough time, to send a rescue team in.

True, the church's one helicopter was sitting in the parking lot, dead in the water, so to speak, and his pilot was dead – literally – but the church had contingencies for this sort of thing. Mostly, the church's loosely-organized "security force" – any group of three or more "bad kids seeking redemption in the Arms of the Lord" – the worse, the better – was used for persuasive tactics when some sinner strayed from the proper path or, in the case of the church's better-heeled constituents, did not make their proper "gift to the Lord Christ" each month. These toughs – Bishop Walker did not know who they were *and he did not want to know who they were*, were scattered all over the South. Each major church district was assigned a "charitable vehicle," a black Hummvee.

The Regulator clock ticked faithfully away.

That *spic* bastard had returned to the room, his rifle at the ready, and his sidearm in the holster at his hip.

"I don't suppose you might be kind enough to hand me back my Citizens Band outfit?"

"You suppose correctly."

"I suppose you're proud of yourself, now that you've allowed me to nearly soil my pants rather than grant me the civil decency of allowing me to walk to the bathroom?"

"You suppose correctly."

"What are you? Some *macho* type who speaks few words like the movie heroes of forty years ago?"

"Yup."

"Enjoy your little bully-boy games for a while longer. It must be no secret to you, that we will soon have more company."

In response, Manuel walked over to Mendelssohn's desk and picked up one of the Cuban cigars he'd lifted, along with the bishop's other immediate possessions, when he'd searched the unconscious prelate a few hours ago. Making an elegant show of passing the cigar under his nose, clipping the end, and lighting up, he puffed contentedly, blowing aromatic smoke in the bishop's face. "I notice you've been glancing at yonder clock more and more often during the past half hour, Bishop Walker." He ambled back over to the executive desk, picked up a heavy silver Rolex watch, and handed it to the bishop. "Wouldn't want to strain your holy eyes, would we? I would think your companions would have arrived by now, don't you, *Excellency*?" Manuel spat out the last word with ill-disguised disgust.

"The roads are not as they should be," Walker responded.

"Where are your forces coming from? Texas? California? We are men of the world, Bishop Walker, so let us speak candidly. Your church is based in the South. Therefore, would it not be correct for me to assume' that the Worldwide Church of Christ would have some minor presence in," Manuel ticked off his fingers, "Birmingham, Montgomery, Mobile, and even Jackson, no more than a three hour drive?"

The bishop grunted, but made no further response.

"It's now been close to four hours since you sent a message for help. Maybe your message didn't get through?"

The bishop grunted again.

"Not to worry, *Preacher*. My *muchachos* are sleeping throughout the building. We want them to be well-rested so they might hospitably greet our guests when they arrive."

∽)∝

"Man, Archie, I've been with the Patrol for twenty years and I've never seen a vehicle beat up like this!"

"Yeah, Paul, it's one gory mess. Christ, it's been a while since I've seen bodies charred this bad. Any ID on any of 'em?"

"I did a quick make on the plates. The Hummvee was registered to the Worldwide Church of Christ in Birmingham. The other car – hard to tell what it even was until I found the plate – was a 1976 Jeep Cherokee registered to one Madison Peebles of Libertyville."

"Were they white or black?"

"When they're burned this badly, they all look the same."

"Any idea how it happened?"

"Best I can make out, there was a bunch a' kids joyridin' in the Hummvee. They probably thought it'd be fun to test it out on this shit excuse for a road, see how fast they could go. That battle wagon leaves pretty good-sized tracks and that one was all over the road, the shoulder, and even into part of the woods. The treads go back about a mile-and-a-half, just outside the Tomkinsville town limits."

"Good thing old Pearlie called in. Might a' takin' us 'til tomorrow afternoon to find this."

"I s'pose. She's the cheapest lookout we have in these parts. Can you imagine what it would be like if someone was driving this road tonight? Prob'ly kill one or two more."

The older officer chuckled mirthlessly. "Only thing I could think of would be two or three more people tryin' to get *out* of Libertyville. Sure as hell no one goin' down there."

"Except that Hummvee."

"It might not even have been headed there. Kids out for a joyride might just have wanted to use this for a two or three mile obstacle course."

"Yeah, and the obstacle that stopped them was an old Jeep and a guy named Madison Peebles. Well, we've done about as much as we can, here. Gotta' do the rest of the drill. Drive down to Libertyville, put up the flashing signs and close off the road 'til morning."

※

"Mordechai, wake up!"

"Huh? Oh, I guess I just dozed off for a moment. What is it?"

"I think I saw some headlights coming from the opposite direction."

"So I'm out on the road again?"

"Uh-huh. I'll turn on the ignition and flash emergency lights."

※

"State Patrol 119, SP 114, over."

"One nineteen."

"Bobby, Archie enroute to Libertyville. I've got an Audi stuck in a ditch three miles south of your position. Driver, passenger, and an old guy who looks pretty sick, might have had a heart attack. Call Triple-A to haul the car and get an ambulance out here ASAP."

"Roger that, Archie, one nineteen."

20

"Well, *Amigos*, let's tote up the score. Three of ours lost, plus the food truck. The old man's out of the picture. The young Reverend is gone. We only got two guests left. We finally got something to eat, but that'll only last us through tomorrow. The bishop promised we'd have some company, but it doesn't look like much is happening. I'm for some shut-eye. How about you guys?"

"Sounds almost too good to be true, *Lider*," José said, "But what do we do with our two guests?"

"On the one hand, we could stand guard over them in shifts, but if – and I say *if* – the bishop's forces ever materialize, every one of us should be as well-rested as possible. Wouldn't you agree, *Reverend*?"

Bishop Walker studiously looked at his fingernails. He refused to even dignify the *Chicano* with an answer.

"José, Hernán, I saw some rope in the storage room adjacent to Mister Peebles' office… "

When the two men returned, they had found four lengths of rope and two sturdy four-legged chairs. "Gentlemen, I realize this is going to be uncomfortable, but I'm sure you understand it's necessary," Manuel said. "Mister Prince, I'm truly sorry to have to discomfort you, but I'm sure you're aware of the position we find ourselves in. Mister Walker …?"

While Manuel kept his rifle trained on Bishop Walker, José and Hernán tied the two prisoners, hand and foot, to the chairs. Then Manuel said, "Gentlemen, I'm sure we can trust you not to leave the office, but if you need anything, we'll be right down to hall in the next room. I bid you each good night."

After the three Hispanics had left, locking the office from the outside, Bishop Walker addressed the other captive. "Mister Prince, let us be honest with each other. We haven't exactly been friends with one another, and I don't perceive we will be friends in the future, but for right now we find ourselves in a similar predicament."

"Yes?" Terry Prince delivered that word in an entirely neutral tone.

"If I am not mistaken, your people hold the written contracts that will transfer this place to Coast Conglomerates in thirty days."

"I'm listening."

"The church is by no means poverty stricken. Would your people be willing to talk if we could go over the figures – and the tax savings to Coast – and make you a deal that might, say, double your investment within thirty additional days?"

"So it all boils down to money, bishop?"

"Doesn't it always boil down to money? The person who has something another person wants badly enough can command the price he wants, to convey it. Plain and simple contract law."

"Plain and simple greed, Mister Walker."

The two men sat, each bound to a chair, in physically uncomfortable silence.

After a while Walker said, "Consider, Mister Prince, you are tied hand and foot to your chair and I am tied hand and foot to my chair. There's no way you can undo the rope that's holding you, because your hands are tied behind your back and there's no way I can undo the rope that's binding me. However, if we can somehow manage to move these chairs so we're back to back, one of us might – I say *might* – have a bit better luck."

"What you suggest could take hours."

"True, Mister Prince, but it's now nine-thirty. Our hosts will probably sleep through the entire night. Let's say they only sleep until four in the morning. That's more than six hours. Or had you planned on doing anything else tonight?"

"And even if we were somehow able to break free?"

"I thought you might be a more percipient man than that, Mister Prince."

"What do you mean?"

"It seems our captors were so smug and sure of themselves that they left the CB radio set on Mister Mendelssohn's desk. …"

~

By midnight, there was the slightest bit of give on the rope binding the bishop's hands. An hour later, Bishop Walker's hands were free.

"What about me?" Prince asked softly.

"I've got to finish *my* job first."

"What do you mean?"

"Just this." Bishop Walker undid the rope binding his ankles and walked toward Mendelssohn's desk. He picked up the mic on the CB set, turned on the lamp near the sofa to its dimmest setting, and sent a much longer message to every regional and district office within a hundred mile radius of the factory. "Forces never arrived at Libertyville cotton works. Request supplemental forces immediately. Front door unlocked. Three officers and nine soldiers in the building. I am on the third floor, Mendelssohn's office. The Hispanic officers are next door, down the hall. Leader calls himself Alcantar. Send serious troops and a replacement helicopter pilot. *Quiet* is the watchword. Walker."

"Okay, Bishop Walker, my turn to be untied."

"That it is, Mister Prince, that it is." The bishop approached the white man, Bible in hand. "Bless you, my son," he said, simultaneously striking Prince sharply on the head, rendering him unconscious. Looking around the room, he found what he was looking for in one of Mendelssohn's drawers, a large handkerchief. He gagged the other man and spoke softly. "You understand, of course, that cooperation only goes so far. I fear if you woke up and were able to find voice, you might prematurely disclose the latest developments to our hosts."

21

At three forty-five next morning, Augustus and Letitia Coyle, who had packed most of their belongings in the trunk of the car the night before, awakened their two daughters, Jennifer, ten, and Kaley, seven.

"Is this the surprise you promised, Daddy?" the older girl asked.

"Yes, honey. It's the surprise of a lifetime."

"Tell us, tell us!" the two girls said, jumping up and down.

"We're going on a big, big trip my darlings."

"Where?"

Letitia put her arms about both children's waists. "Our whole family is going across the country. All the way to California! Do you know where that is?"

"Oooh, yes!" shrieked Jennifer. "That's where Mickey Mouse lives and Snow White and the Seven Dwarfs, and ..."

"That's right, honey," said Augustus. "We're leaving right now. We'll be driving all day today and then for three days after that. Five days from now we're going to visit Disneyland!"

"Isn't that in Florida, Daddy?" Jennifer said.

"No, honey, you're thinking about *Disney World*. *Disneyland* is the place where it all started."

"Are we moving away from here?"

Letitia took over. "Yes, girls. Daddy and mommy are moving to San Diego, which is a great big city in California, where it's sunny just about every day of the year. We're going to build a wonderful new life together."

"That's very far away," Kaley spoke up hesitantly.

"Yes it is, darling," Augustus replied.

"Is grandma going to come with us?"

"Not for a while, but when things settle down, grandma and grandpa, and even grandma Rose will come to visit."

"Are you going to work at a new church, Daddy?"

"No, honey," said Letitia. "Daddy's been a preacher long enough. He's going to get a whole new kind of job when we get to California. He'll get to spend much more time with us."

"I want grandma to come *now*!" Kaley whined.

"Darling, there's not enough room in the car for all of us *and* grandma, too."

"Well," Kaley said resignedly, "she is pretty fat. When we get to California, can I have a kitten?"

Augustus looked at Letitia lovingly. He'd always believed kids could adapt to anything, and his daughters were as eager and excited as he'd hoped they'd be. They'd made arrangements with Letitia's parents to ship their meager store of household goods to San Diego in two weeks. By that time he was confident they'd find a place to stay and he'd find a good job, certainly a better paying job than he'd had in Libertyville. He looked at his watch. "Five minutes to four, everyone. Time to get rolling if we want to cross the mighty Mississippi by this afternoon."

"I know how to spell Mississippi," Jennifer said proudly. "I learned it in school. M-I-S-S-I … S-S-I-P-P-I."

"Aren't you the smartest girl in the world!" Letitia said, hugging her oldest daughter tighter.

CHAPTER 21

"What about me?" wailed Kaley. "I'm smart, too!"

"Yes you are," Augustus said. "You're so smart I'm going to let *you* be the one to choose the kitten."

⊱⊰

Just after four that morning, there was a slight rustling noise at the front of the building. Manuel did not hear it. The remainder of the Hispanic troops slept in various rooms throughout the building. If any of them heard the noise, they felt it was nothing more than the wind.

Bishop Walker, who had dozed lightly during the night, rose from the couch, went over, looked out the third story window, and nodded in satisfaction. He counted twelve men as they exited from three nondescript Land Rovers, all of them armed. These were not the ragtag forces the church gathered up on a moment's notice to quell minor disturbances. These men were highly disciplined regular employees of the church. Whatever had gone wrong with the first phalanx, the power that Bishop William Wyatt Walker wielded was such that the church would not tolerate a second mistake.

The church's troops entered the building one at a time, in virtual silence. No one noticed the late model Honda Accord driving west on Libertyville Road, just east of the cotton works.

⊱⊰

The girls had fallen asleep in the back seat less than five minutes after the Coyles left the house. As they turned onto Libertyville Road, Augustus said softly, "Going to pass the cotton works in about two minutes. I can't believe how quickly things moved after the bishop did what he did. I suppose in my heart I owe him a vote of thanks."

"Darling, to paraphrase the old refrain from *Fiddler on the Roof*, 'May the Lord bless and keep the bishop ... *far away from us!*'"

"Amen!" Augustus said, chuckling. As they passed the cotton works, Augustus saw something that looked very much out of place – a dozen armed men in camouflage entering the building.

"You see it, too?" Letitia asked quietly.

"Uh-huh. Seems awfully strange to me."

"I agree, Augustus, but it's not your battle anymore."

"You're right," he said resignedly, and kept driving.

※

Inside the building, one pair of ears on the second floor heard the commotion and one pair of eyes saw a number of armed strangers coming through the door. Fulgencio Arenal crept quietly down the hall, where he alerted the two other men who'd been sleeping in the room farthest from the stairwell.

※

The armed Black troops trudged up to the third floor. Two of them stood by what they'd been told was the boss's door and two of them stood immediately outside the door to the adjacent office. At a nod from the team leader, four others retraced their steps to the second floor. The remaining quartet descended to the ground floor. The eight troops on the lower floors were detailed to search for and dispatch the nine Hispanic soldiers they'd been told were sleeping there.

※

"I can't get rid of this feeling, darling," Augustus said, an hour later. "Something tells me the bishop got through to somebody and something terribly wrong's going to happen at the factory."

CHAPTER 21

"I wouldn't put it past him. If you're having trouble with your conscience, why not call 9-1-1 and report what you saw?"

"Good idea, Letitia. The state police are in the best position to sort out the good guys from the bad guys." He punched in three numbers on his cell phone. The call was answered a split second latter. "9-1-1, go ahead."

"9-1-1, this is Reverend Augustus Coyle of the Worldwide Church of Christ in Libertyville. My family and I are going on holiday. We got an early start. As we were driving west on the Libertyville Road, we saw a dozen armed men entering the old Libertyville cotton works at about four-thirty a.m. I don't know what's going on there, but it looked very strange to us."

"What is your present position?"

"Eight miles west of Libertyville. We're driving a 1986 Honda Accord, license number 5NKF835."

"Thank you for your call, Reverend Coyle. I'll relay your message to the appropriate authorities. Have a good holiday, sir."

ഓൽ

"State Police? 9-1-1, Elaine Harding. A Reverend Augustus Coyle reports suspicious activity, Libertyville cotton works. Here's the recording."

After listening, the state police intake operator said, "Thank you, 9-1-1. We'll dispatch four vehicles to investigate. Nearest state patrol office is Tomkinsville. The Ops Center is in Montgomery, two hours out. Happy Sunday."

ഓൽ

"Good morning, Mister Alcantar. It appears that you and your two friends are now the guests of the Worldwide Church of Christ. If you will please move quietly down the hall to Mister Mendelssohn's office and be kind enough to unlock the door, it will hopefully be unnecessary for us to use these weapons. I request that all three of you leave your weapons on the floor and come with me."

A similar scene was repeated on the first floor as the four African-American troops awakened the half dozen sleeping Hispanics in a large anteroom and ordered them to lay down their arms.

The church forces on the second floor were not so lucky. Fulgencio Arenal had positioned the Hispanics in a triangular pattern, so that when the church's agents arrived at the far end of the hall they were suddenly ambushed from the rear. "Into the clerk's room, *pronto*," Fulgencio ordered. It took less than five minutes for the Hispanics to bind and gag the surprised Blacks and relieve them of their weapons, two of which were submachine guns. Fulgencio directed one of his men to stand guard over the African-Americans while he and his associate quietly moved back down the corridor toward the stairway.

"It seems we are now *your* hosts. Mister Alcantar," the bishop said, beaming. "I trust you had a nice rest. I hope you don't have to urinate too badly, since you will be treated with the same courtesy you afforded me."

This time it was Manuel's turn to remain silent. The pressure on his bladder was immense, but he wouldn't give the scurvy cleric the pleasure of watching him squirm.

"Let us count the numbers," the bishop continued. "Three of you, the Anglo, who doesn't count either way, and five Brothers, four of whom are armed. Since you three have regrettably abandoned your weapons in the other room, the odds are now rather one-sided the other way, wouldn't you say?"

José started to say something, thought the better of it, then sat down.

CHAPTER 21

"Mister Walker – "

"*Bishop* Walker, or Your Excellency, or better yet, I prefer the term 'Your Grace,' which you used when we first met."

"Mister Walker," Manuel continued. "I am going to go into the bathroom where I will urinate. I will not embarrass myself by soiling my pants, nor will I splash the floor with my waste in the corner of the office. If your goons want to kill me, that's their prerogative." He stood and headed toward the toilet.

The bishop tried to block his way, but Manuel shoved him to the side and continued walking. Two of the African guards raised and cocked their rifles, but the bishop stopped them by raising his left hand. When Manuel returned, the bishop said, "Your act may have seemed brave to your associates, but it was simply foolhardy by any objective standard. You are fortunate that I am in a charitable mood this morning." He looked at his wristwatch. "Five o'clock. Any of the rest of you have to go pee-pee? I see you all do. Very well. Better I extend you the courtesy than that this whole office smells of your detestable urine."

When José, Hernán, and Prince returned from the bathroom, Bishop Walker directed them to the armchairs and the sofa. He sat in Mendelssohn's chair, facing the four of them.

"All right, my friends, the meeting is called to order. Four guns have voted me chairman and I accept their unanimous vote. Does anyone have anything to say to open the conversation? No one? Very well. I will take the floor.

"Gentlemen, we'll use the carrot and stick approach. Mister Prince, we'll offer you the carrot. According to my calculations, I estimate that Coast Conglomerates is into this project for three million dollars. Obviously, it'll be much less if the old man dies sooner rather than later, and it appears he might do that. The other old fellow, Mister Peebles, won't be far behind. So let's knock a half million off the equation. Two-

and-a-half million. The big attraction to Coast is not the amount of the outlay, but the amount of the tax incentives and the good will you'll generate with the government. The value of the package is six mil. Am I close?"

When Prince said nothing, Bishop Walker continued, "I'll assume my ballpark guess is fairly accurate. The church is willing to pay you ten million dollars in cash plus five percent of the net proceeds from our operation of God's Country for five years. Don't look so shocked at our generosity, Mister Prince. Your own accountants will confirm we'd spend more than that paying taxes. I suggest you take that offer back to your superiors."

"No security?"

"Security? When we're paying one hundred percent of the price up front? I don't think so."

"I mean for the five percent of the net."

"The church is a 501c (3) nonprofit corporation. Your company will get a copy of the federal tax return and the check for five percent concurrently. That'll be in the contract."

"What about the free housing we promised the employees? Their pension and profit sharing benefits?"

"Like the title of the book – *Gone with the Wind*. Oh, we'll build lodgings all right. Who wouldn't want to stay overnight in God's Country? We may charge a bit more than you were thinking of charging."

"And the town?"

"Also like the book."

"So you'd kill a hundred-fifty-year-old town, just like that?"

"Mister Prince," the bishop said patiently, "oak trees die, pine trees die, people die, and towns die. Nothing lasts forever. This sad excuse

CHAPTER 21

for a town has been diseased and dying for the last twenty years. We're just giving it a fitting burial. Like the Phoenix of old, the Lord will create a new town, a better town, *God's* town, from the ashes. Well?"

"I'll give it some thought."

"That's not good enough, Mister Prince. I will afford you a chance to call your superiors later this morning. I expect an answer today."

"Can't do it, bishop," Prince said. "Today's Sunday, not a legal day to do business, even if I could reach my superiors."

"I think you can if you really try hard, Mister Prince." The bishop walked over to the smaller man, grabbed his right pinkie finger and started to push it back slowly. The Coast Conglomerates representative winced in pain. The bishop signaled one of the African-American gunmen, who handed him a hunting knife. "If I don't get the answer I want by three o'clock this afternoon, we'll start by sending your president your two pinkie fingers, which will be of no further use to you by that time. Two quick chops and you'll be minus two fingers. No matter, it's not a dangerous proceeding and one of my associates will quickly stanch the blood."

"What about us?" Manuel snarled at the bishop.

"We've offered the carrot to Mister Prince. I fear we can only offer you the stick."

22

"You're a lucky man, Mister Mendelssohn. The doctor says it was only a very mild heart attack. You survived because you're in the best shape of any sixty-nine year old she's ever seen."

"What's the prognosis?"

"Quite good, Uncle Moses," Sarah said. "A baby aspirin, twenty milligrams of Crestor and ten of Zetia a day. They'll want to look at you every four months for the first year, and every six months thereafter. They said you made the right decision to sell the cotton works, 'cause you don't need the stress."

"Maybe, but the jury's still out on who I sold it to. Damn, I'm sorry about Madison. 'Course, he was on a long, slow decline. Things would only have gotten worse, and he might have gotten Alzheimers or senile dementia. Can you imagine, waking up every morning knowing how bright you were and knowing you had lost it all?"

"Isn't that a bit maudlin, Uncle Moses?"

"No, it's simply the truth. At least Madison bought the farm while he still had his wits about him. The lucky thing is he died so quickly he didn't even know he'd been killed. No illness, no pain, just a real quick sleep, one, two, three, and it was over. It's the same with younger people, too."

"What do you mean, Mister Mendelssohn?"

CHAPTER 22

"Take you, Mister Ben Zvi. Would you have preferred that your Sylvia lingered on as she did, watching her die a little more every day, all the while knowing there was not a damned thing you could do for her, or would you rather she had died instantly in a car crash, or giving birth, or in some other totally unexpected way?"

"That's an impossible question to answer."

"Is it?" The old man leaned back, took a sip of water, and continued "When it came to Sylvia, it was impossible for *you* to let go because *you* wanted to hold on to her as long as you could, even if it meant that *her* suffering was prolonged. Don't raise your hand in denial, Rabbi, I'm not standing in judgment, I'm only speaking a terrible truth, but a universal one. When someone goes on a trip or moves away to a distant town, it's always harder for the one left behind."

Their reverie was interrupted. "Breakfast, Mister Mendelssohn," the morning orderly said, in that bubbly, over-the-top cheeriness that is somehow pandemic to health care professionals on the morning shift. "You're going to love this."

Moses Mendelssohn looked down at the tray. One piece of pumpernickel toast, half an orange, and a cup of green tea. "Lovely," he muttered. "No bacon?"

"It's not on the menu for you this morning," she said. "Oh, I just *knew* you would like your breakfast. I'm so glad we're feeling better this morning."

"We? I didn't know you were feeling ill."

The orderly, who was already out the door and on the way to her next patient, didn't even hear him.

"I refuse to be selfish," Mendelssohn said. "This serving is so generous I insist we divide it three ways."

❧

"The stick?"

"You and your filthy Mexican gang-bangers are out of here, Mister Alcantar. We release your people two at a time. Two of my associates will escort each of them to one of our vehicles. They will be driven to various places of our choosing and from there they will be discharged to go hence."

"A remote spot off the road where your people will kill them?"

"Most likely. The lucky ones will live to fight another day, provided they get through the underbrush and the snakes. You have what, a dozen men here?"

Manuel remained silent.

"Whether you answer or not does not concern me, *Pancho*," the bishop said, dropping all pretense of civility. "The Brothers have already flushed them out and are making sure they're as comfortable as can be expected."

"And if we don't go along with your plan?"

In answer, the bishop nodded at one of his troops. The African-American lifted the gun, aimed at Hernán's head, and blasted away.

"Now there is one less to dispose of. Whom do you want to be next? It isn't going to be you, *Pancho*. Since you're the leader, we'll save you for last, so you can assume full responsibility for the death of your *compadres* and watch one by one as they all fall down."

"You're supposed to be a man of God."

"Ah, such logical reasoning," Bishop Walker responded, laughing bitterly. "Our Muslim friends from the Middle East to Indonesia are fighting in the Army of Allah and they believe they will achieve heaven if they die killing others in the service of their God. We Christians, who know *our* God is better than *their* God, don't hesitate to walk into their countries and celebrate the numbers we put up on a scoreboard of how many 'ragheads' they kill. How many of *my* people did the good, white *European* Americans enslave over the centuries? How many Native Americans did they slaughter for the greater glory of the Christian God?" Yes, Mister Alcantar, we are, all of us, men of God."

"I trust there is no room for negotiation."

"None. Perhaps I'll give you one small concession. You may choose the order in which your friends leave the premises."

෧෬

"We haven't heard any message canceling the 9-1-1 call," Paul said to his partner. "Montgomery wasn't all that excited about it, but they said we should meet 'em at Libertyville cotton works at nine-thirty. Can you imagine, sending four cars and a SWAT team from Montgomery to Libertyville on a Sunday morning? You'd think they might have something better to do with the governor's money."

"I agree. Most likely they're going to use the call as a readiness exercise. Even if there was anything going on there, it would have been over a long time by now."

23

Ten minutes ago, the bishop's forces had taken the second two Hispanics to the Land Rover. With Hernán's death, that meant there were less than half of Manuel's forces left. No matter what the odds, his people were now substantially outnumbered.

Bishop Walker said, "Gentlemen, I fear I'm now getting quite hungry. One would hope, Mister Alcantar, that your friends had the good grace to leave some of last night's food. I need to stretch my legs a little bit. With your permission, or without it, I shall adjourn to the second floor cafeteria. Franklin, would you be kind enough to accompany me? I believe that three of our number can easily handle the two men left in this room."

Manuel listened with a growing sense of loss as Walker and his subordinate descended the stairs.

At that moment, Fulgencio Arenal, who was ensconced on the second floor, said to his comrades, "We have been without food long enough. I'm going to scrounge us up some coffee and breakfast. Make sure you keep an eye on our nasty friends." He carried a submachine gun he had seized from one of the invaders as he started toward the cafeteria.

In Mendelssohn's office, the three guards and their prisoners jumped when they heard the *rat-a-tat-tat* of the submachine gun being fired. Lucius Jackson, the replacement helicopter pilot, calmed his nervous associates down. "We're the only ones who came in here with machine guns," he said. "They're probably just showing off, giving Bishop Walker a twenty-one gun salute." A moment later, his confidence sagged when he heard a scream, followed by a loud, gasping moan.

Walker's escort had been killed. Bishop Walker had taken a slug in the knee and one in the groin and gone down like a sack of potatoes. Of the twelve Blacks who'd come into the building four hours before, two were driving the Hispanics to their destiny, one had been killed by Fulgencio Arenal's submachine gun blast, and three were being held prisoner in the far room on the second floor. That left six Black troops in the building, three in Mendelssohn's office and the other three on the ground floor.

Of the Mexicans left in the building, two were guarding the African-Americans on the second floor, Fulgencio was roaming the area, and Manuel and José, although disarmed for the moment, must still be considered potentially active. Six to three, but it could shortly become six to five. The odds were becoming more even.

Fulgencio ran down the hall to summon his two armed associates.

ஐ)ରେ

The Land Rover, headed west on the Libertyville Road, was just pulling off the surface to discharge one of the two Hispanics when the officer driving a state patrol cruiser saw it and became suspicious. A late model Land Rover with two African-Americans and two Hispanics on a Sunday morning was not normal. Maybe this would be more than an exercise after all.

The driver radioed his position. The patrolman sitting on the passenger side jumped out of the cruiser, his sidearm drawn, and pointed at the African-American driver. The loudspeaker from the cruiser cut through the morning silence. "Everyone exit the vehicle immediately, with your hands on top of your heads! I repeat, all of you exit the Land Rover *immediately*!"

❧☙

"In local news, Madison Peebles, sixty-nine, a widower from Libertyville was killed in an automobile accident on the Libertyville-Tomkinsville Road last night at about 9:00 p.m. Details of the accident and the names of the other victims are unconfirmed."

"Awww, no," Roy Kemp moaned, badly shaken by the news broadcast from Tomkinsville. He pulled over and buried his face in his hands. He thought, with more than a shred of guilt, *It could have been me. I could have gone with him on that trip.*

When he'd pulled off to the side of the road, he thought, *It wouldn't hurt anybody if I passed by the cotton works before church to make sure everything's all right.*

❧☙

Fulgencio entered the room to find all five men in a state of nervous agitation. "*Dos Negroes*," he told his companions. "One of them with a gun." He sliced his right forefinger from left to right along his throat. "No more. Other fellow, old, fat guy, no gun, he's sitting at bottom of stairs, not going anywhere soon."

"We're gonna' have a real war," one of the two armed men said. "We got three prisoners here. I say we kill 'em off now. Battle casualties."

One of the African-American men shook his head violently, clearly agitated. Fulgencio calmly walked over and removed his gag. "You wanna' say something, *Negrón*?"

"Yessir," the man said. "We got called early this morning. Nobody said what it was, we were just following orders. I suppose you're the same?"

CHAPTER 23

Fulgencio nodded.

"I got a wife and four small children at home in Montgomery," the prisoner continued. "I'm barely makin' ends meet. I'm thirty-one years old. Name's Oscar Denham. I took this job 'cause I needed the extra money. Please, sir, I'm not ready to die."

Fulgencio was moved by his simple statement and the dignity with which the plea was made. Something in the way the man spoke had the ring of truth to it. "What proof do you have that if we don't kill you, you'll try to break free and kill us?" "You've got the guns. Think, man, even if we got loose we'd have to overpower you to get the weapons back, and chances are that more than one of us would die."

"What do you propose?"

The Black man thought for a moment. "How about this? I've got the keys to one of the cars. You cut us loose. Before you do, search us one at a time to make sure we don't carry any concealed weapons. Walk the three of us out to the car, we leave and we don't come back."

"Sounds good in theory, *Amigo*," Fulgencio said, "but how can I trust you won't grab some guns in the nearest town and come straight back here?"

"Honestly, sir, I don't know. You're Mexican, I'm Black. The two cultures have never liked or trusted one another. Maybe this is the time to start."

"What's in it for us?"

"Three less enemy."

"How many of you are there?"

"Twelve of us came in from Montgomery this morning."

"That cuts your number by one-quarter. Still … tell you what," Fulgencio said. "I'll try what you suggest. Maybe one of us will come up with an idea between now and the time the three of you are in the car."

Moments later, Fulgencio left the room with the first of the prisoners. They were halfway down the hall when two of the three Black troops on the ground floor stormed up the stairs toward the sound of the shots and the grievously moaning bishop. Without a second thought, Fulgencio coolly fired the submachine gun again. The two African-Americans spun round and collapsed in their death throes.

෴

"What was that?" Lucius shouted.

"Sounds like we got a war going on downstairs," José said calmly.

"But we ambushed all of you when we first came in," the replacement pilot said lamely.

"Maybe you missed one or two."

Lucius looked uncertain. In the absence of the bishop, he'd been designated the team leader. He had the distinct feeling things were starting to unravel. Five minutes had elapsed. Bishop Walker hadn't returned. He looked at his two other gunmen.

"Bobby, you wanna' go outside and see what's goin' down?" The younger man hesitated a moment. "That wasn't a request m'man, that was a command."

"Are you sure, Mister Jackson? That'll only leave two of you in the room against two of them and the Anglo."

"We can handle it, Bobby. I'm not asking you to go on a suicide mission. Just look around and report back."

෴

CHAPTER 23

As Fulgencio continued downstairs with his prisoner, the last of the three Black men who'd been stationed on the ground floor came into the front hall weaponless, his arms raised. It took less than a minute for the Brother from the second floor to explain what was going on.

"This ain't *my* war, either," the African-American said. "I don't mind joining the other three in the car, Mister Fulgencio."

There was a slight shuffling sound from above them. As the Mexican and the two Blacks looked up, they could not believe what they saw. The bishop had somehow managed to slide over to where the two Brothers had been killed and grabbed one of their submachine guns. With a mingled look of intense pain, malice, and terminal rage, he fired indiscriminately into the three men at the bottom of the stairs, killing all of them instantly.

※

Moments later, a badly rattled Bobby, obviously frightened out of his wits, returned to Mendelssohn's office.

"Well?"

"It's a b-b-b-blood bath, Mister Jackson. The bishop's sitting at the top of the stairs on the second floor with a submachine gun. He's badly hurt. T-t-there's f-f-f-four of ours dead and one Mexican."

"Calm down, Bobby. Just do the arithmetic. A dozen of us came in. Two are out driving two Mexicans to kingdom come. That leaves ten. Take away four and that leaves six plus the bishop, all armed. Against these two," he said, nodding in the direction of Manuel and José, "and they don't pose a threat."

※

Meanwhile, on the second floor, Fulgencio's two companions, hearing the gunfire, had come running out, leaving their two prisoners still bound. They watched in horror as the bishop, still cradling the submachine gun in his arms, rocked back and forth, moaning incomprehensible rubbish. So in agony was Bishop Walker that he did not hear them approach. Coming upon him from the rear, one of the Hispanics shoved him with a booted foot, and the bishop rolled down the stairs. The additional pain and shock rendered the cleric unconscious.

The Mexicans quickly went back to the room and unbound their hostages. The conversation was brief. "A lot of dead bodies out there, including the guy who decided to free you. We expect you'll keep your part of the bargain."

The Blacks nodded vigorously. "Very well, then. Our fallen comrade gave you his word and we will honor it." When they reached the bottom of the stairs, the Hispanic who'd addressed them said, "Which one's your man? You'll forgive me, but I can't tell. You *Negroes* all look alike to me. He's probably got the keys in his pocket and I don't think you can drive very far without them."

Moments later, they walked out into a dry but gloomy day, just as Roy Kemp was pulling into the parking lot.

"Hey, *Gringo*!" one of the Mexicans hailed him.

"Well, hello yourself. Are you one of Mister Braganza's guys?" The Hispanic looked confused. "You know, the guy who was here negotiating with old man Mendelssohn yesterday. I heard one of you calling him '*lider*' or something like that?"

"Oh!" the Hispanic said, brightening, "you mean Maximilian Bragado-Galba y Alcantar."

"Yeah, that sounds about right."

"Are you the guy that was with him?"

"No, Señor, that must have been one of the others."

"Oh. Well, sorry, but you Mexicans all look alike to me."

"Who are you?"

"Roy Kemp, the night watchman."

"Mister Kemp, can we ask you a favor, *por favor?*"

"Shoot."

"Our two friends got lost on the way to Montgomery. Could you give them directions to help them get there?"

"Don't see why not. You guys lookin' to get to Montgomery?" The two Blacks nodded. "Drive outta' the parkin' lot, turn left and head west on the Libertyville Road. I'll follow you for a coupla' miles to make sure you got it right. When you get to the main highway, turn left and follow the signs."

సాఇ

When the Land Rover had taken off, the two *soldados* returned to the building.

"It's very quiet, *amigo*, isn't it?"

"*Si*, like everyone's sleeping or maybe dead."

"If there's anything going on, it's up on the third floor. I haven't seen or heard from Manuel all morning."

"He might be in trouble. Maybe if we look upstairs..."

24

"What was that, Mister Jackson?"

"Probably your imagination, Bobby." Lucius looked out the third floor window. "Shit! That's not anyone's imagination. Two of the Brothers just drove off in one of the Land Rovers. What the fuck is going on here?"

"For someone who's in control, you look awfully shaky," Manuel said. "You think maybe something's gone wrong?"

"Watch it, *spic*," the pilot said. "You seem to forget we've got the guns."

"I'm not forgetting, *Negrón*," Manuel said, egging the African-American on. "What kind of army you got where everyone shoots everyone else? Doesn't seem unified to me."

"Shut the fuck up, asshole! You got that?"

"Do I detect a little bit of temper?"

"You got a hearing problem, *Pancho*?"

Manuel stood up and approached the pilot, fists closed. The Black team leader raised his rifle menacingly. "One step closer, *Pancho*. Just one step."

"Gentlemen," Terry Prince spoke up. "This is insanity. Stop it right now!"

CHAPTER 24

"And just who do you think you are to order me around, Honky?" Lucius Jackson growled disdainfully.

"Don't you see, you guys are at a stalemate? What kind of foolishness is this? Last man standing wins?" He was furious, and his fury propelled the little man beyond the fear he'd initially felt. The other four men in the room looked at him with various degrees of attention, ranging from curiosity to outright contempt.

"Stop being an idiot!" Prince shouted, his control giving way. "The only winner in this game is going to be *no one*. There are no winners and there can't be any winners."

"Even with those deserters gone, we're down to four plus the bishop against – "

"Yes, go on," Terry Prince said. "Four against how many?"

"Two unarmed Mexicans."

"Perhaps, but that assumes all of your men were killed by *your men*. You may talk bravely to keep up your own confidence, but do you really believe all that shooting came from *only* your side?" Lucius looked uncertain. "Did it ever occur to you that your men might have missed a couple of men? Or maybe a couple of your men *might* have been ambushed by Mister Bragado's men?"

"Or maybe Bishop Walker might have been shot by one of *your* men or Bishop Walker was only shooting at *your* men?" This from José.

"And now it truly is a stalemate, Señores." The two Hispanic men from the second floor entered Mendelssohn's office with a flourish. The five men stood facing each other, weapons drawn and aimed at one another. They stood that way for what seemed like an eternity, but which was probably only a few seconds.

Finally, it was Manuel who broke the silence. "So it's come down to this. A deadly chess game with human pieces. Three to two armed pawns, two unarmed Hispanics, one unarmed Anglo, and an aptly named wounded black bishop, somewhere in the building, whom any experienced chess player would say is effectively pinned. Eight pieces left out of an original group of thirty-two. Gentlemen, I'd say we're at end game."

"Maybe we should put our weapons down and discuss this," said Lucius.

"Good thought, Mister Jackson, but who's going to be first to lay down his weapon? You don't trust us, we don't trust you. You fool me once, shame on you, you fool me twice, shame on me. So I can't see that idea working."

"Why don't we let Mister Prince leave the game?" José asked. "He's got no stake in this and he's not out to hurt anyone."

"Except he's the only hostage who counts," Lucius said. "He's the guy with the piece of paper that says his company gets all the chips. Once again the *Niggers* and the *Beaners* suck hind tit. Once again the Anglos hand the little guys their asses on a platter."

"So I'm an expendable hostage, Mister Jackson?" Prince spoke up. "First your bishop wants to cut my fingers off, now that's not enough for him. If you kill me, what have you gained?"

There was silence in the room. Finally Lucius spoke. "Personal satisfaction."

"You'll get lots of that when they fry your ass in the electric chair," Manuel said. "If you're even around that long. I don't see any of my people putting down their weapons. Whoever fires first, *someone's* gonna' make sure that at least *someone* from the other side isn't left standing. Isn't that the way a chess game works?"

"OK, *Pancho*, let's say the white guy goes. How does that solve *our* problem?"

"It doesn't. But it lets the players who have the stake decide how it gets solved."

At that moment, everyone in the room heard a loud crash downstairs at the front of the building. The usually calm Lucius was so unnerved by the sound that he accidentally discharged his weapon, instantly killing Manuel.

One of the two Mexicans, believing Lucius had killed the *lider* deliberately, fired at Lucius from short range, just as Bobby rammed into the Mexican. The burst of fire from the submachine gun barely missed Lucius, but caromed into Terry Prince, pulping Prince's head and ending his life.

"Freeze! Everyone down on the floor!" The leader of the SWAT team fanned his automatic from one side of the room to the other. Three shots were fired in unison. The first brought down the SWAT leader, the second extinguished Bobby, and the last killed José.

That left two Mexicans and two Blacks standing. With the exception of Lucius, three of the men were so low on the totem pole that no one even knew their names. A second SWAT team member, seeing his comrade shot in cold blood, dispensed each of the three.

"Wait, officer! Hold your fire!" Lucius said. "I can explain everything."

"Who are you?" growled the SWAT man.

"Lucius Jackson, *Sir*, First Sergeant USMC, Retired. I have my ID with me if you want to see it."

The officer looked around at the grisly sight in the room. The SWAT man had seen a lot in his fifteen years with the State Police, but this was as ugly as it got. "My God! What in the hell happened?"

"I am employed by the Worldwide Church of Christ," Lucius said. "As best I can make out, Bishop William Wyatt Walker was taken prisoner and held hostage by a group of armed men last night, when he came to assist the local pastor, Reverend Coyle, negotiate for the purchase of this factory and the surrounding forty acres."

"That's consistent with our information," a second voice said. It belonged to the patrol lieutenant. "9-1-1 received a call from someone identifying himself as Reverend Augustus Coyle this morning at 0445. There's a large man lying at the bottom of the stairs," he continued. "He's very badly hurt."

"That's Bishop Walker," Lucius said.

"Somebody needs to get him to a hospital immediately," the lieutenant said.

"Now, isn't that a coincidence?" Lucius replied, smiling for the first time since the police had arrived. "The bishop was able to free himself from his captors just long enough to send an emergency message to church headquarters. Apparently, the invaders murdered the helicopter pilot who'd flown the bishop here from Birmingham. He left word to send a replacement helicopter pilot with our delegation, and I happen to be the guy who got the call."

"So that explains the chopper sitting in the parking lot?"

"Guess so, Lieutenant."

"Well, Mister Jackson, I can't say 'All's well that ends well,' but it looks like the good guys won. I suppose you'll want to ferry the bishop out to the nearest major hospital."

"That's probably the best solution, Lieutenant. I only thank God it ended this way."

"I'll put a call in to the state patrol office in Tomkinsville. They'll have the dubious honor of sending a cleanup crew down. Your bishop's a pretty big fellow. It'll take four or five of us to get him into the helicopter. We've got a pole-and-canvas carrier if that'll help."

"Thank you, Lieutenant. I appreciate all the help I can get. I only hope the keys to the chopper are somewhere nearby, where we can find them."

CHAPTER 24

As the men accompanied Lucius Jackson downstairs and loaded Bishop Walker onto the travois, the Bishop awoke to consciousness and looked straight into the lieutenant's eyes. "My, my," he said. "An African-American lieutenant. Praise be to the good Lord that America has come this far that one of our own has ascended to such high rank. What is your name, Son?"

"Charles, Your Excellency. Charles Wright."

"Well, Lieutenant Charles Wright, you have my eternal thanks and my blessing. As soon as I am healed and I return to my national radio broadcast, I will publicly thank you and, of course, I will not wait that long to commend you to your superiors."

"Why, thank you, Bishop Walker," the lieutenant said, almost fawning with delight. "Men," he said, addressing his police unit, "let's help this great and good man into the helicopter."

When they got to the helicopter, providence would have it that the door was unlocked and a key was already in the ignition.

"Where will you be taking him, Mister Jackson?"

"Montgomery's Baptist Medical Center, one of the best trauma units in the area. It's less than an hour's flight from here."

"Very good, sir. Have a safe flight. God bless."

"Thank you, Lieutenant Wright."

The rotor started up slowly, then spun faster and faster, creating a flow of air and a screaming noise that drove the policemen to the shelter of their cars. When Lieutenant Wright and his second in command were safely inside their patrol cruiser and the sound of the whirling engines was muted by the closed windows, Wright's subordinate said, "Sir, that was one of the most awful experiences I've had in all my years on the force."

"It is, indeed, Sergeant. And yet, with his wounds and all, that bishop is one of the most courageous men I've ever met. You know,

Sergeant Taylor, I somehow feel as though I was truly in the presence of one of God's anointed."

The police cars pulled slowly away, moments before the helicopter lifted off the tarmac. Lucius Jackson pulled back the yoke and the great red-and-white bird lifted smoothly into the air.

They'd been aloft less than thirty seconds when a huge, unexpected gust of wind grabbed the helicopter and slammed it into the Libertyville cotton works. The helicopter exploded on impact. There were no survivors.

EPILOGUE

Six of them sat around the large conference table at the attorneys' commodious conference room. Joyce Emmett, President and CEO of Coast Conglomerates had greeted Moses with unabashed warmth when he, his niece Sarah, and Rabbi Mordechai ben Zvi entered the room together.

"You feeling better, Moses?"

"Yes, Joyce, quite a bit, thank you. It was very kind of you to send flowers, although, to tell you the truth, a nice Kosher salami would have been appreciated."

"Goldblum's will send you a case of them next week."

"I said 'appreciated' not *allowed*. Can you believe it, one salami sandwich on the first year anniversary of the heart attack, not before?" He mock-scowled. "Seriously, Joyce, I can't tell you how thankful I am that Coast agreed to renegotiate the contract."

"Moses, it's actually a better deal for us. We pay considerably less, we get the same tax benefits, and we come out, you should pardon the expression, 'white as the driven snow.'"

"All right, let's make sure we've got it down right." Bruce Greenbaum, Mendelssohn's attorney, deferred to Tom Benson, the Bentley Adamson partner assigned to handle the details of the amendment.

"Thanks, Bruce. Number one, same cash-for-lifetime deal for Mister Mendelssohn as before. Number two, we dispense with the monetary arrangements for the late Mister Peebles. Number three, in lieu of the benefits to Mister Peebles, Coast will purchase an additional forty acres immediately outside the perimeter of the property and deed that property to the Moses Mendelssohn Irrevocable Living Trust. We understand that the way the Trust is set up, the lifetime beneficiary is Moses Mendelssohn and the remainder beneficiary is *Gan Sylvia Memorial Egg Ranch, Incorporated*. Have I got that correct?"

"You do," Greenbaum affirmed.

"Aside from that, everything remains as it was?"

"It does."

"All right, we've been over the contract many times before. The amendment is just a page-and-a-half. You've all read it. Are we in agreement?"

Everyone at the table nodded solemnly.

"Well," said Tom Benson. "Let's get it signed and break out the champagne."

ಸಃಡ

The white Audi stopped in front of Moses Mendelssohn's home. Sarah and Mordechai exited the car. Moses came out onto the porch to greet them. The late February sun heralded an early spring, but Moses had learned over the years not to trust the weather in Libertyville.

"So you're really going to do it, Mordechai?"

"Yes, Moses," he said, embracing the older man. "This has been my dream since Sylvia died and a little piece of her will always be here. I've given my notice to the school and my notice to *Chabad*. They were generous enough to send out a large number of laying hens and a dozen young people who've committed to work for next to nothing for the first year. And our president has generously donated eight industrial-size coops to start the thing going."

CHAPTER EPILOGUE

"You're going to be the general manager?"

"That I am."

"And Sarah?"

"What better resumé for national marketing manager than a degree in the humanities and a professorship in medieval studies?"

"Delightful," the old man said, sardonically. "Here I am, comfortably in my dotage, when I should be relaxing on the beach in southern Florida, and I'm taking on the job of president of this company? I should live so long."

"You should live to a hundred and twenty, Uncle Moses. Besides, what are you *kvetching* about? You've only signed on for two years."

"I'm worried about our West Coast Rep," Moses intoned gravely. "Here we are, a *Jewish* company and we're represented to the world by a ... a *Schvartze*? Whoever thought I'd see the day?"

"Uncle Moses, you are such a damned hypocrite!" Sarah said, laughing. "You were *partners* with a Black man for sixty years. He was your closest friend in the world!"

"I suppose you're right." He shrugged . "Still ... an ex-Rabbi, an ex-professor, and now an ex-preacher man! What is this world coming to?"

"That I don't know, Moses," Mordechai said. "Who knows? Maybe this town *will* come back to life. Maybe we'll succeed beyond our wildest hopes and maybe we'll fail beyond our worst fears. But it's just like the world. We go from defeat to defeat to defeat, but maybe we'll ultimately achieve a victory of sorts. We'll never know 'til we try, will we?"

THE END

A List of the author's books published by Samuel Wachtman's Sons

Skorzeny: Dancing with the Devil (2017)

The Wrecking Crew (2016)

The Politics of Insanity (2016)

Arcade: The Ultimate Chameleon (2015)

Assassin - The Ultimate Thriller (2014)

Legacy - The Birth of Modern Turkey (2013)

Amazing Grace: The Story of Grace O'Malley the Notorious Pirate Woman (2012)

Billy Jenkins: Europe's King of the Cowboys (2012)

Scribe - The Story of the Only Female Pope (2012)

Against All Odds - The Magnificent Trio That Built the Israeli Air Force (2012)

The Politics of Hate - A Piercing Insight into American Politics (2012)

Made in the USA
Columbia, SC
12 November 2018